DEATH, SLEEP & THE TRAVELER

BY JOHN HAWKES

Charivari (in *Lunar Landscapes*)

The Cannibal

The Beetle Leg

The Goose on the Grave & The Owl
    (also in *Lunar Landscapes*)

The Lime Twig

Second Skin

The Innocent Party (plays)

Lunar Landscapes (stories & short novels)

The Blood Oranges

Death, Sleep & the Traveler

JOHN HAWKES

DEATH, SLEEP & THE TRAVELER

A New Directions Book

Portions of this work appeared in somewhat different form in *Ameri-
can Review*, *Antaeus*, and *Fiction*, to the editors of which grateful
acknowledgment is made.

Death, Sleep & the Traveler is titled after a work of sculpture by
Aristedes Stavrolakes, who died in 1962 at the age of thirty-five.

Manufactured in the United States of America.
First published clothbound by New Directions in 1974
(ISBN: 0–8112–0522–3).
Published simultaneously in Canada by McClelland & Stewart, Ltd.

New Directions Books are published for James Laughlin
by New Directions Publishing Corporation,
333 Sixth Avenue, New York 10014

Designed by Gertrude Huston: photographs by Dennis Martin.

For Kitty and Philip Finkelpearl

DEATH, SLEEP & THE TRAVELER

Ursula is leaving. Dressed in her severe gray suit, her gardening hat, her girdle, her negligee, her sullen silk dress, her black blouse, her stockings, her red pumps, and carrying a carefully packed straw suitcase in either hand, thus she is leaving me.

She is going at last not because of what occurred on the ship or because of the trial, which has long since been swallowed into the wet coils of its own conclusion, but because I am, after all, a Hollander. With her skirts awry, her elegant tight black military coat draped to within inches of her ankles, and with her hair blowing, the black bun sculpted at the back of her head, a cigarette lighted between pale fingers, and with belted valises lightly in hand, thus she is leaving—because she does not like the

1

Dutch. Yes, Ursula is going off to find somebody very different from myself. An African, she says, or a moody Greek. If she had not forced me to board the white ship alone, perhaps we would still be at peace with one another. But soon she will no longer exist for me, nor I for her, and when she passes through the front door I shall be standing alone in the kitchen with one hand motionless on an enameled tile and my broad soft face pressed to the window glass. For a moment I will glimpse her car, which she will be driving or which someone else will be driving, and then my wife will be gone.

Why did she come to my support at the trial only to desert me in the end? Why did she wait this long to tell me that I am incapable of emotional response and that she cannot bear my nationality? Why did she refuse to join me on the white ship and so abandon me to death, sleep, and the anguish of lonely travel? Surely it was more than her boredom and distaste for shipboard games. Perhaps there was another man. Perhaps he will soon be sitting at the wheel of my wife's car.

For me there is only the taste of cold water, the sensation of glass against my heavy cheek, and the sound of waves.

✳

In the darkness the ship was rolling like a bottle lying on its side in a sea of oil. Sweating in the night's heat, feeling in the flesh of my forearms the warmth of the ship's rail, and puffing on my small Dutch cigar and staring down at the phosphorescent messages breeding and rippling in the black waves, suddenly I knew the ship was making no forward progress whatsoever. The knowledge was startling. One moment I was sweating and smoking at the ship's rail, the most reluctant voyager ever to depart on a cruise for pleasure, and the next I was leaning at the polished rail in sudden possession of the sure knowledge that the ship, though rolling, was otherwise standing still, or at best imperceptibly drifting. How could it be?

I smelled the salt that burdened the night sea air as well as the ocean in which we lay, I saw the shooting phosphorous below and, not far from my left shoulder, a thick skin of dew drawn to the contours of the prow of a white lifeboat. I heard the persistent rhythm of a tapping wireless key in the darkness. And yet I knew that the ship had stopped. But why? How? Even cruise ships, no matter how directionless, were under obligation to maintain steam and at least minimum forward motion on the high seas. To stop, to lose headway, could only put the vessel in gravest danger. And then a hand touched my sleeve, a voice spoke, and my freshly lighted cigar went sizzling down to quick extinction in the night sea.

"Allert," the young woman said, "won't you join me and the other passengers for dancing in the dining saloon?"

⌘

My Dutch name rendered in English is Alan. But in Dutch, and despite the accent on the first syllable, my name is clearly a repository for the English word "alert," as if the name is a thousand-year-old clay receptacle with paranoia curled in the shape of a child's skeleton inside. I myself have always been quietly alert.

⌘

"Peter," I said to my oldest and closest friend, "I wish that now, after all these years, you would take her regularly to bed. She expects it of you, she expects it of all men, she wants you to make a strong and consistent overture. Force her to more than yielding. She spends her life pouting and smoldering and waiting for opportunities to yield. But once committed she is an extremely active lover, the kind of woman who causes suicide. And she likes you. We have both made that perfectly clear already."

I placed my cigar in the glazed white earthen ash tray, looked at my friend and smiled. Behind his back and through the broad windows the late sun was streaking across the snow for miles. At that moment Ursula, my wife, entered the room and sprawled in a white leather chair in such a way as to reveal to my friend and me the tender fat of her upper thighs as well as the promise of her casually concealed mystery. It occurred to me then that my friend and wife were perhaps more intimately agreeable with each other than I had thought. But it did no harm to urge Peter toward the inevitable, even if he had long since discovered it.

"Ursula," I said, "do you know what we have been talking about?"

She rested her cheek in the palm of her hand, allowed the other to fall against the full white barely visible crotch of her underpants, and looked across the room at me with heat in her eyes. Even from where I sat I could smell the soap and sourness between her heavy legs. The mere thought in my mind was making her moist.

Later she decided that I needed to embark alone on a quest for pleasure.

4

⌘

Around my navel there is concentrated a circular red rash. At first a few isolated splotchy areas of pebbled crimson, it now consists of a broad red welted ring completely encircling the little untouched island of the navel. The fungus, which is what it must be, surely, is textured like the outer livid flesh of a wet strawberry, and is spreading. Soon its faintly exuding and yet sensationless growth will blanket the entire surface of my global belly. Perhaps I contracted the infecting seed while lying almost naked on the lip of the ship's pool and watching beneath the shield of my crossed arms the slowly tanning figure of the young woman who later confronted me once in her stateroom with a goat's horned skull masking her sex.

⌘

The approaching extinction of what we have known together is unavoidable, not at all like an amputation, and certainly not a matter of morality. Ursula does not like my name, my large size, my self-control, my superficial national characteristics, my cigar smoking, my dreams, my affectionate attachment to a certain city in Holland, my preoccupation with the myths and actual practices of sexuality, my benevolence, my sense of humor which, like the more enticing elements of human anatomy, emerges only on the rarest occasion brightly and bedecked in green. She dislikes me most, she says, for my failure to respond to her emotionally. I, in my turn, resent and admire her constant smoldering, resent and admire her lassitude which is sexual invitation, and resent and admire her boredom which is denial. There are times when I dislike more than anything in the world the lazy fit of the top of her stocking around her upraised thigh as well as the thickness of her breasts, her small waist, the breadth of her stomach, the terrible harmony between her wandering body and her impregnable mind. I do not like her egocentricity, her psychological brutality, her soft voice, her harsh personal judgments, her awareness of sexual challenge, her habit of fondling her own rough nipples, her patience, her cleverness, her occasional smile, her weeks of depression. And yet we have given each other freedom, excitement, tenderness and comfort. We have shared a long marriage.

⌘

I awoke. The porthole was half open and, in the moonlight, was streaked with salt. But so too were my lips, the clothes piled on the nearby chair and flung on the floor, the sheet that was stiff and the color of silver on our two bodies. Salt-encrusted and bitter, all of it, as if we had slept through a violent storm with the porthole open.

I was awake, my left leg was bent in cramp, the body next to me was small, the cabin was not mine. The darkness, the glint of a brass hook near the louvered door, the girl whose naked sleep I could feel but not see, and the salt, the moonlight, all of it made me more than ever convinced that the small unfamiliar stateroom in which we lay had momentarily been emptied of black sea water. The pillow was damp. But what else? What else?

"Good God," I whispered, "good God, we have stopped again. The ship is not moving."

She murmured something and curled closer, her smallness and youth and nudity lay cradled in the darkness against my rigid and now sweating chest and thighs. I felt her tiny wet tongue licking my finger. But the ship was without lights, that much I knew, and was untended in a sea so calm that not the slightest tremor climbed the delicate white iron plates to suggest to me, the now conscious and alerted sleeper, even the minimal reality of the vast tide. No tapping of the wireless key, no messages from the ship's half-drunken vibraphone player. Nothing. All around me I felt the empty decks, the empty lifeboats, the schism between the rising moon and the black tide. And I struggled unsuccessfully to comprehend a fear I had never known in my past life. No doubt the problem concerned two cosmic entities, I told myself: the sea, which was incomprehensible, and the ship, which was also incomprehensible in a mechanical fashion but which, further, was suddenly purposeless and hence meaningless in the potentially destructive night. Eliminate even the most arbitrary of purposes in such a situation, or from the confluence of two cosmic entities, I told myself, and the result is panic.

"Listen," I whispered, "it's happening again. The ship is not moving."

In the darkness, lying bulky and naked in a strange bed, tasting the salt and feeling the stasis of the ship in my own large body, in these circumstances I knew it was unreasonable to speak as I had in fact just spoken to the girl at my side. And yet there was nothing I could do but pour my cigar-drenched breath across her small sleeping face. I felt exactly like one of those naval officers waiting, in former times, for the inevitable arrival of the torpedo

7

speeding through the black night. The young woman had herself selected me from all the passengers, also she had already been more friendly to me than anyone I had ever known, and in her smallness appeared capable of bearing any amount of pain or fear my presence might inflict on her. Given all this I felt oddly justified in looking to the helpless girl for immediate and practical relief. But waiting, listening, suffering the cramp in my leg, and utterly conscious of my total identification with the dead ship, nothing could have prevented my urgent whispering in any case.

"We are becalmed," I whispered. "I must go on deck."

She curled still closer and spoke though she was quite asleep. Then she took nearly half of my finger into her mouth. Suddenly, marvelously, I understood what she had said and felt through all my weight and cold musculature the heavy slow rumble of the engines and the unmistakable revolutions of the great brass propeller blades in the depths below us. The distant vibrations were all around us, were inside me, as if my own intestinal center was pulsating with pure oceanic motion and the absolute certainty of the navigational mind doing its dependable work. Our arms were crossed, my fingers were tentative yet firm, the girl's dreams were in my mouth. But the sea, I realized quite suddenly, was not calm, as I had thought, but rough.

⌘

"Allert," Ursula was saying, "the trouble with you is that you are a psychic invalid. You have no feeling. I wish that just once you might become truly obsessional. If you

8

were obsessed I might at least find you interesting." But Ursula was wrong. I am not some kind of psychic casualty. It is simply that I want to please, want to exist, want others to exist with me, but find it difficult to believe in the set and characters on the stage. Then too I am extremely interested in failure.

But why is she leaving?

✳

The sun was filling the dining saloon, the whiteness of the ship was everywhere. The enormous plate-glass windows that were sparkling, the white cloth on our table for eight, the broad green tiles of the floor of the dining saloon in which we waited at the second sitting for luncheon, the crystal and silverware and even the white dress uniform of the young wireless officer sitting coarsely beside me, in all this the whiteness of the ship and brilliance of the sun were evident. It was a period of perfect light, shortly after the second luncheon gong on a clear day, and beyond the frivolous yet pleasing insularity of the dining saloon the ship's motion was remarkably measured in singing cables, a taut flag on the prow, the pleasingly uneven faint undulations of the sharp prow against the unmoving fictional horizon. And from our stern the froth of our unmistakable wake was purely devolving in the long white choppy path of our disappearing nautical speed, all of which at the moment I knew full well, since for exactly an hour prior to the second luncheon gong I had stood alone on the ship's stern and drunk deep of the glare and wind and salty taste of our powerful but fading passage.

The menu announced consommé from shallow silver

cups, and had it not been for the printed menu as well as for the recollection of my hour at the taffrail, I doubt that I could have sat a moment longer at my first impending meal at our table for eight. At the instant of this realization I imagined the consommé before us, each silver cup bearing its garnish of water cress like a green island drifting in an amber sea, and in that instant I took my florid face out of the menu, felt my armpits growing suddenly dry, and smiled in turn at most of the other members seated at our somewhat isolated table.

The girl whom Ursula had pointed out to me the previous day was, ironically enough, seated exactly opposite the young ship's officer at my side, so hence almost exactly opposite from me. Like the rest of them she was studying her menu. Her long-stemmed water glass was empty; with a sudden mild intensity I noted that the coarse young wireless officer was fishing for the girl's small sandaled foot with his poorly polished white shoe. I resented his action, I moved to rearrange the napkin spread in my lap. The water, like the consommé, had not yet appeared. The girl must have noticed my concern because in the next brief passage of time, as I broke through the frozen glassy crust of a roll with my two thumbs, she looked at me directly as if she were about to smile. Her eyelashes made me think of flies climbing a wall.

"I am Dutch, not Swiss," I said in answer to someone's question. "But in my case it is a common mistake."

The ship veered slightly, the sun flashed, two black-jacketed men began setting before us the low flat silver tureens filled with the tepid consommé and green garnishes and puckering chunks of lemon. I admitted to myself that the soup deserved some sort of public comment.

"This consommé," I said quietly, "has been siphoned from the backs of lumbering tortoises whose pathetic shells have been drilled for the tubes."

The silence, the singing of the crystal, the plash of water filling the goblets, the bent heads, the sun on the naked shoulders of the girl who was wearing pants and a halter, all this told me that I should not have spoken, should not have revealed in hyperbole my loneliness, my distaste for travel, my ambiguous feelings about the girl. Again I glanced beneath the table and saw that the carelessly daubed white shoe was now pressed against the girl's very small and naked foot. The girl, in the motions of her arch and toes, was encouraging the attention of the young wireless officer and even responding to his touch.

The girl's halter was tight, triangular and dark blue over what it covered of her childish chest. The cuff of the wireless officer's white tunic sleeve was frayed, and not only frayed but unclean, stained by a smudge of some substance pertaining to his job as wireless operator. The girl was ordinary yet unfamiliar, while the officer was a common type, a careless black-haired young man who singled out one special girl for himself on each aimless cruise. I knew his type and was not surprised to see that the coarse fingers of his right hand were constantly shifting my silver fork or brushing the rim of my waiting plate. As his secreted right foot performed its seduction, so his visible right hand had to give offense, and both for the sake of the girl who was seated across from us and watching.

Spoon to lip, eyes meeting those of the young girl at an odd angle, conscious of a high wide transparent wave of spray beyond the nearest sheet of plate glass, and seeing the varied faint colors in the fine spray, and hearing a few notes of the vibraphone, suddenly I realized that the officer's effrontery was going to be far more extensive than I had imagined. His hand left the table. His hand slipped from the table in such a way as to engage my attention but not that of anyone else. In order to thrust his hand into the pocket of the wrinkled white tunic, he moved so that his bent elbow touched my heavy unobtrusive arm. Intentionally. For an instant I speculated about the girl's age, I heard a saxophone barking distantly, I thought of the two great ponderous black anchors wet and dripping where they hung bolted like monolithic torture instruments to the high prow of the ship.

"Tomorrow we reach land," the officer said to the girl while continuing to feel about slowly in his pocket and to invade my luncheon hour with the deliberate tip of his elbow.

"So soon? I thought we wouldn't see anything for days."

"First port of call tomorrow. There'll be horses and carriages for sightseeing."

I felt again the insistent elbow. I glanced down. I saw the man's hand cupped palm upward on his thigh, the hand crudely tilted in my direction, the small glossy faded yellow photograph cupped and shining in his hand. I frowned, the girl was smiling, I returned the spoon to the bowl. I glanced down at what was obviously an example of very old-fashioned pornography. The fissured celluloid and two small white gelatinous figures were cupped in the man's hand, framed in his palm, and now the young man was laughing at the girl and twisting, winking his stubby little antique picture as if he expected me to take it in thumb and forefinger and transfer it surreptitiously to my own white pocket. He began to make a brushing motion with his rude thumb across the two small stilted nudes as if wiping away some invisible film of dust. I put down my napkin, pushed back my chair, excused myself.

"Tomorrow," said the girl as I got to my feet, "will you join us in one of the carriages?"

"Thank you," I answered in my thickest accent, "perhaps."

The ship was softly undulating, with knife and fork in hand the young officer was beginning to eat his luncheon. I spent the next day in my cabin waiting, listening to the noise of temporary disembarkation, feeling the heat of land, feeling the timbers of the pier through the ship's steel, thinking that the thick yellow hawser visible beyond my porthole was to the stilled ship what a life preserver was to the floundering man. At least the hawser made sense of our immobility.

✖

There were gongs, there were whistles, there were blasts from high-pitched pipes, screams of compressed air. Even from where Ursula and I stood together on the crowded deck near the gangway I could see that the ship was high and sharp and clear, a paint-smelling flowered

13

mirage of imminent departure over the lip of the earth.

"You see," said Ursula into my ear and laughing, nodding in the direction of the young woman leaning happily at the ship's rail, "you will not be alone, Allert. Not for long."

I turned, I looked again at the young woman who was leaning on the rail and smiling at the crowd on the pier, at the loading shed, at the other ships in the harbor, at the smoke rising more swiftly and blackly now from the pale blue smokestacks above our heads. The girl was standing with no one, she waved but not to anyone in particular down on the pier. And when I turned back to Ursula our own ship's whistle blew, its vibration filling deck, sea, sky, bones, breasts, and tearing us all loose from the familiar shore.

"She'll take care of you," Ursula shouted into my waiting ear, "you'll see."

⌘

In my dream there is a table of rough wooden planks, darkness, another person, light coming from nowhere, and in the center of the table a pile of shining wet blood-purple grapes in a clay bowl. We are outdoors and I feel no apprehension. And yet it seems to me that the grapes, which are clearly at the center of this late-night timeless experience, are somehow moving faintly of their own accord. The air is without wind, without stars. The grapes are waiting, massed in a curious faint motion. The other person, who is female and stands well beyond the edge of the table, is not inviting me to approach the grapes, though she is

14

standing beyond the table only in expectation that I will do so. Yes, I am aware of the other person and pleased at the sight of the heap of grapes with their tight wet skins and reddening color. But then there is a change in mood, a change in perspective, because now I am standing beside the table in the warm night air and noticing that the grapes are unlike any I have ever seen, since each grape grows not from the single short tough stem which is part of the usual cluster, but is instead attached top and bottom by tender almost transparent tubes to its neighbor. Yes, the grapes are heaped in the bowl in a single tangled coil rather than in familiar bunches. And now I see that these grapes are larger than usual, that their slick skins are watery red, that they are definitely moving against each other, that they are stretched and twisted into oddly elongated shapes instead of the usual spheres, and all because each grape contains a tiny reddish fetus about the size of the tip of my thumb.

The grapes are transparent, I see the fetuses, the other person has drawn appreciably closer to watch my reaction to the grapes which are wriggling now like a heap of worms. Despite their pale redness they are still purple. Despite their distorted shapes they are still glistening and large. But when a handful is separated wetly from the rest of the pile and is suddenly half crushed on the wooden surface of the table (by the other person who is clearly my wife), I am revolted and unable to eat.

When I told this dream to Ursula she asked me how anyone could be so afraid of life as to dream such a disgusting dream.

We sailed from Amsterdam, from Bremen, from Brest, from Marseilles, from farther north, from farther south, from Amsterdam. The brochure describing the voyage lay on the table beside my chair for weeks before the day of departure. I smelled the sweet smell of dust hours before we first sighted land when I went to my cabin. Ursula waved me off from the crowded pier. There was no one to wave off the girl at the rail. I had no interest in boarding that ship. I did not want to sit beside Ursula and drive to the pier. I was not attracted to severance, sun, sea, the geography of separation and islands and unexpected encounters in cabins like mausoleums. I did not want to float in the ship's pool which was a parody of the sea it traveled on. I did not want to sail. But the return was worst of all since by then the girl was gone. I plan never again to look at the rough sea though I am filled with it, like a sewn-up skin with salt.

In my dream I am somehow endowed with the rare North Penis, as if the points of the compass have become reliable indicators of sexual potency with north lying at the maximum end of the scale. First I see the phrase *North Penis* on a sign above the door of a shabby restaurant which I recognize as a place that serves good wine, and then I am seated at the single unsteady little table in front of the restaurant and am aware of the sudden ill-fit of my trousers and of the physical sensations of the rare North Penis between my legs. The waiter is scowling, there is no

16

way to share my embarrassment and secret gratification, I am forced to drink a half glass of the excellent wine alone.

When I told this dream to Ursula she made no comment but instead leaned across to me enigmatically and put her hand on my thigh. Later in the day she said she found the explicit sexual insecurity of my dream surprising, but would tell me no more.

※

"Allert," she said, "all men wish occasionally to be free of their wives. You really must go on this cruise. And go alone."

She was facing away from me and toward the large expanding glass pane of the window, so that beyond her naked back and beyond the window the snow spread westward in a dazzling white crust for miles.

※

The third musician was playing his vibraphone with naked knuckles, with knuckles split to the bone and bleeding onto his sentimental percussive instrument. We were heading into a darkening choppy westward sunset. I went out on deck.

※

It was so cold that a skin of ice had already formed on the surface of Peter's bright blue car that was still faintly steaming at the side door of his week-end house in the country. The setting sun was licking the hard bright machine like some great invisible beast on its knees.

17

"Ursula, for you," he said, giving her the glass. "And for you, Allert. A quick drink and then we'll try the new sauna."

"Cheers," I said in my native Dutch and saw the hard wet light of the sun, which was just beginning to set, in the frozen lacquer of the car beyond the window, in the metallic sheen of Peter's gray hair, in the window glass itself and in our tumblers, our eyes, our breaths still visible even inside the essentially unused house. Peter lit the enormous fire, we drank, the three small valises—two of matching straw and one of stiffly shining hide—stood together in the entrance hall. The fireplace smelled of the damp soot of the wintry forest, Ursula was sipping from her glass and smiling.

"All right, my dears," Peter said, "I have a treat for you."

He refilled the tumblers, he brought the bottle, so that outside the cold and the fierce declining light leapt as one to tumblers and fingers, to bottle and fusing voices, so that the car and the house and the three of us were all cut from the same timeless stuff of light and ice. We laughed, we stumbled together in single file, Peter pointed the way with the bottle held out before him by its frozen neck, though the path was clear enough. The sun turned suddenly orange on the haunch of Ursula's tight trousers, for some reason the sound of my own footsteps made me think of those of a lurching murderer. Unmarked, faintly visible, the path covered the short distance from the house above us to the cabin in the little cove below in spectacular fashion, skirting the bare birches and crusted snow to our

18

right and hooking downward to the edge of the black and brackish sea on our left.

The cove was narrow in the mouth but deep, a perfect little fat pouch cut roundly into the rocks and snow of that frozen coast, and in the very center of the cove stood the cabin freshly built of stripped white logs and smelling of wood chips and tar and creosote. There were no windows, the large plank door was locked with an obviously new padlock, and yet greenish and highly scented smoke was drifting up from the chimney. The naked birches of the hillside crowded down the white incline to the cabin, which had been built only a few feet from the round rocks, the edge of ice, the brutally black salt water. It seemed to me that all the rocks, large and small, were the color and texture of a man's skull long exposed to snow, sun, rain.

"Peter," I called, smelling the green smoke, the fresh wood, and feeling the tension between the white trees and snow and the black water, "what a perfect spot for a sauna!"

The door closed behind us like the door of an ice-house, as if it were six or eight inches thick. Ursula and I commented on the sense of well-being that filled the little solidly built log cabin. The interior smelled of cedar, of ferns, of polished rocks, of water. Over everything drifted the scent of eucalyptus trees.

"Ursula," Peter said, "why don't you use the dressing room first? Then Allert and I will take our turn."

She put down her tumbler and disappeared. She returned with her torso wrapped in a white towel. For only a moment or two Peter and I left her alone tilting the cold glass to her lips and watching fragile cords of flame binding themselves tightly about the log glowing in the enormous fireplace. It took us only a moment or two to strip down and hang our clothes on the wooden pegs as Ursula had done, and to wrap ourselves in the heavy terry cloth towels. One of Peter's black socks dropped to the floor. Ursula's clothes were bunched in silken shapelessness on the wooden peg.

"You look like a pair of old Romans," she said, and the three of us clinked together our tumblers hard, with gusto. Ursula had removed her jewelry and, clearly enough, was pleased to be standing between Peter and me in her white towel. She was holding the upper edge of her towel with a soft hand.

"Yes, Peter," I said, "it was clever of you to locate all this sensual isolation in the very midst of so much magnificent desolation."

"But this is only the beginning, my friend. You'll see."

And then quietly, seriously, peacefully, we entered the sauna. The rose-colored light, the flagstone floor, the walls of cedar planking, the tranquility of the intense heat, the now heady smell of eucalyptus, suddenly the power of this kind of languid confinement was far more considerable than I had thought.

"Actually," Peter said, "it is best to spread the towels on the benches and then to sit or lie on them."

Ursula loosened her towel, removed it, placed it on the hot wooden slats between Peter and me, and slowly leaned back against the cedar wall with her knees to her chin. Her knees were together only for comfort, just as her heels for the same reason were spread apart, and her eyes were open and level while her lips, her heavy lips, were agreeably relaxed. She did not intend to hide her breasts with her knees though she was doing so. Already there was appearing on the cellulous density of Ursula's body a heat rash indistinguishable from the rough discoloration of the sex rash that was so periodically familiar on her chest and neck. I knew at once that Ursula was thinking and at the same time pleasantly daydreaming in the intense heat.

Peter and I spread our towels, he assuming a perfectly upright Yoga position to Ursula's right, I reclining into a half-leaning position to her left. Already the rose-colored light had dimmed perceptibly, while time had disappeared completely in the intense heat. Back straight, abdominal muscles visibly tight, ankles crossed, hands on spread knees, in this way Peter had turned himself into a living religious artifact constructed only for the sake of the receptacle that was his lap. And in the receptacle of Peter's lap lay the hunched conglomerate of his still dormant sexual organs.

My friend did not move except occasionally to lick his lips. Ursula was slack and motionless. I lay massively sprawled with my forearm on the towel, my hip against Ursula, my large smooth shoulder propped against the cedar wall. Our eyes were dry, our skin was dry, with all the clarity of a peaceful dream our immobility was giving way in slow motion to fragments of action: Peter ladling oil of eucalyptus onto hot rocks; Ursula smiling at the bland rear view of Peter's nudity and thrusting a dry hand between her thighs; I shifting and rolling onto my back with knees raised and feet flat to the towel and hands clasped beneath my head; Peter turning with ladle in hand; Ursula reaching down more firmly, more gently, and pleasing herself with one finger, with several; Peter resuming his Yoga position; Peter ladling out the oil of distant trees; I placing the flat of my right foot against Ursula's hip; Peter sitting again with his hands on his knees and his spine in a curve; Ursula placing her heels together and then spreading wide her knees and arms toward Peter, toward me.

"We must plunge into the water," Peter said. "We must not wait too long."

"The first naked man I ever saw," Ursula said, "had a cock down to his knees."

"We'll cleanse the skin, finally," Peter said, "with birch branches."

"But the word is Dutch," I heard myself saying, drunkenly, serenely, "not Latin."

The room was dry. Our bodies were dry. The heat was high enough to stimulate visions, to bring death. The oil of eucalyptus was running, was forming a slick film on walls and floor, was greasing our nipples and turning to thick foam between our legs—though invisibly, silently. I lay again on my back and closed my eyes and listened. Of all the women I had known, only Ursula made that muted popping sound in the midst of all the other sounds of oral passion, and now in the timeless heat of Peter's sauna I heard Ursula's own sound and then, aware of Peter and Ursula tangling and untangling, the one rounding upward her sweet back, the other throwing high his chin as if to crack his trachea from within, and then aware of silence sliding among us like a pool of oil, suddenly I felt the

22

muted fierce sensation of Ursula who had turned around quite naturally to me.

Felt and heard the tip of the tongue, the edge of the tongue, the flat of the tongue, the softness inside the lips, the resilience of the lips firmly compressed, the gusts of unsmiling breath, the passionate suction of the popping that was sensation as well as sound, the nick of a white tooth, the tip of her nose, the side of her cheek, the feeling of her head on its side with the mouth gripping me, carrying me, as a dog carries a sacred stick, until I felt that last moment of Ursula's wet concentration—tender, vibrant, brokenly rhythmical—and then felt myself disgorging, disengaging, sinking, curling slowly into a gigantic ball like some enormous happy animal armed with quills.

It was Peter who saved us in time, who kissed Ursula's roughened mouth just in time, who swatted her sharply on the flank just in time, who pulled me out of my stuporous imitation of the woodchuck just in time, who caught hold of Ursula's nude body and mine and dragged us out of the sauna and into the frozen sunset and leaping and laughing into the shocking blackness of the salty choppy water just in time to prevent irreparable burns or internal damage or even death. And in time also to revive us, to wound us back to life in the bright light, the unbearable coldness, the crunching of the thin ice that made small bleeding cuts on our naked feet and ankles.

Heavy, lumbering, laughing, exposed in shock, down we crashed into the mid-winter tide and hurt our arches on the round rocks and even chased each other with handfuls of virgin snow. We revived, we shook, the rash on Ursula's upper body was like a vivid red tapestry on a white field. Our fragments of speech, our sounds of choking laughter, our sounds of flesh slapping flesh all broke across the last light and last silence of the frozen day.

Back in the cabin to which we fled to escape the sea, the cold, the pure ominous light, and to retrieve our clothes, Ursula engaged in a prolonged sexual embrace first with Peter and then with me in front of the logs that were still burning as brightly as before. In front of the fire we redeemed each other's scars and restored to cold bodies the comfort of familiar warmth. We were not in a mood for the birch branches.

It was later, when climbing up the crusted path in the darkness, that I received my all-too-accurate premonition that Peter's life was going to end, when that moment came, in the sauna.

⌘

"Yes, Allert," she said, "I am going to find somebody very different from you. An African, perhaps, or a moody Greek. And I shall never again submit to marriage."

⌘

I went immediately to my own cabin, by tracking the numbers on the louvered doors. I would allow no one else to carry my new valise. I found the door, I entered and placed the valise on the little unsteady luggage stand. I shut the porthole, I locked the door, I sat down on the edge of the bed facing the valise and resting my forearms on my thighs. I waited, I stared at the valise, I listened. In the midst of motion I could not visualize, and the silence that followed the whistles, the shouts, the crush of human activity and the subliminal grinding of iron wheels and greasy gears, slowly I became aware of the stabilizing throb and purpose of the engines far below and knew that we were under way and sailing.

Nonetheless, I was unable to make myself open the valise. I was unable to open it, in fact, for several days, which no doubt accounted for my unshaven appearance at the earlier meals.

Strapped, locked, made of bright golden leather, my new valise sat untouched on its flimsy stand for several days, a pedestrian Pandora's box filled, I thought, with the sentimental or useful objects of my traveling self. During those hours while I sat on the edge of the tightly made up bed and stared at the fattened valise, often I asked myself if Ursula had thought of a cruise deliberately, since long ago the two of us had shared this kind of cruise in celebration of our recent marriage.

Finally I unpacked the valise.

⌘

I am a person who drinks inordinate amounts of cold water. When I rise and stand on the warm tiles in my silk pajamas, or when I pause at our kitchen sink which lies like an enormous ceramic trough beneath the window facing the rear of the driveway down which Ursula will soon depart, or when I return to our house from feeding the geese on our small artificial pond, or when I wake in the night or turn away from the window with the western

25

exposure or think of Ursula lying somewhere above me with her magazine and expanding plans, in each case inevitably and deliberately I pause and fill a thick clear glass with cold water which, slowly and fully, I drink down. I taste the water as it comes from under the black flat rocks, I taste the icy water flowing down a river of light, I am aware of it chilling my teeth and refreshing me. Each glass of water causes me to breathe deeply, to grow a shade more somber, to anticipate more keenly the taste of the little cigar with which I follow each pure glass of cold water. And I have insisted on my dozen or so glasses of water each day throughout all of the last ten years or so of our long marriage. I drink only water and an occasional schnapps whereas most of my fellow countrymen drink beer. And still, as Ursula says, I am forever bloated.

But there is no image or analogy with which to evoke the taste of water, which happens to correspond to the view I hold generally of life. The thought of salt water is unbearable to me. My desire for fresh water is increasing daily. I number myself among those few men who are able to admit that their thirst is unquenchable.

⌘

"Allert," Peter said, "what do you think of my theory that a man remains a virgin until he has committed murder?"

⌘

There were two life jackets stored on the top shelf of the narrow closet in my cabin. Staring into the closet that was nearly empty except for the life jackets, and also staring into the mirror fastened to the inside of the closet door, in this way I saw myself in the mirror in my undershorts. I imagined myself strapped into one of the orange jackets, I thought of myself tying the white cords in the darkness of a night at sea. It pleased me to think that I had lost track of time.

And yet the sight of two life jackets caused me a certain uneasiness, as did the two pillows on the bed, the two chairs covered with flowered chintz, the smell of soap and sea air in the cabin, the absence of anything personal in this cabin that was obviously intended for two persons but occupied by only one. I did not wish the company of the other shipboard passengers, and yet I believed that I would never feel at home in a stateroom with so much false decoration and from which some second unknown person was forever missing.

I replaced one of the white cords that was dangling. I dropped my shorts, I felt the humming of the ship in the soles of my feet, I prepared myself in trunks, straw slippers, dark glasses and white terry cloth robe for a session at the edge of the ship's pool. I drank from the plastic glass-lined flask of ice water. I studied myself through the large black lenses of the sunglasses.

Then I left my cabin. I took my towel, my straw hat, my book, and even as I detoured down to the deck below instead of walking directly to the pool that was situated on my own deck in the aft of the ship, I found myself distrusting what appeared to be the monotony of the ship's steady course. The curious levitation I felt in the softly lit corridor was sure to give way to some abrupt shock or a sudden diminution of forward speed and then a pause and then the terrible pull of the propellers churning in reverse. A clear day was no guarantee against the diving and rising monsters of the deep.

The length of the corridor was spanned underfoot by a thin rubber mat and overhead by a series of muted light bulbs in steel cages. A fire axe was bolted to the bulkhead behind a sheet of glass. I could hear my slippers marking my solitary progress down the corridor. Through the thickly-smoked lenses of my dark glasses the details of the corridor were so darkly obliterated that it might have been leading me through some unfamiliar hotel or through the severe structure of a bad dream, except that the corridor was not level, following as it did the contours of the white hull, and in the very nuclear substance of its steel plates was filled with all the physical by-products of the stresses of what could be nothing other than a ship in motion on a flat sea.

Her cabin door was open. Hardly able to see my way, smelling fresh paint and the grease of electrical cables and the fresh lingering scent of my recent shower, I knew immediately that her cabin door was open, not hooked partially ajar with a brass hook as were many of the doors I passed, but standing fully open so that I could not help but see the partially opened porthole, the pen and loose sheets of paper on the writing desk, the archaic typewriter, the orange beach robe flung on a chair, the small and still dripping swim suit dangling from one of the thick brass ring-bolts around the porthole. I could not help but see the wireless officer half propped on the unmade bed in his tunic and undershorts, and see also the young woman who, dressed in a boy's white undershirt and a pair of tight blue denim pants, was standing before a small ironing board and pressing what were obviously the wireless officer's white trousers.

Her hair was still damp. Her rump was a little sectioned fruit in the tight blue pants, her feet were bare, her energetic upper body was like a child's. The wireless officer was reading something, a book or magazine, on her unmade bed. She was ironing his white trousers as if to do so were a commonplace of both the past and present.

When I again reached the upper deck I reversed my direction, shunned the pool, and returned to my cabin where in robe and slippers and dark glasses I lay flat on the flowered bedspread that was stretching like a sterile skin across my empty bed.

I was unable to read. Only considerable inner concentration prevented me from donning one of the orange life jackets over my white robe.

✻

He was at my side. The moonlight was on the rail, on the deck, on the waves and foam below us, and the wireless officer was at my side. One of his white shoes was hooked on a lower rung of the ship's rail.

"Sometimes, when a man is in the winter of life," he said, "he begins to find young women attractive. He begins to pursue younger and younger women. He intrudes where he is not wanted. He finds himself unable to seduce the girl away from the younger man. He attempts unsuccessfully to be their friend, burning all the while only to touch the girl. He makes a fool of himself."

I thought of the moonlight turning the sea's black salt to silver, for an instant I saw the crumpled white uniform streaked with algae. In the moonlight he was picking his fingernails with a small bone-colored cuticle stick.

"If you think I am in the winter of life, as you put it," I said, suppressing my anger, "you are mistaken. Very much mistaken."

✻

"Allert," Peter said, breathing his frozen breath into the silence between us, "I would like to take you up on your suggestion. Do you remember?"

In woolen socks and rubber boots cut off at the knee and with silver-barreled shotguns cradled in our arms that were bent and stuffed with warm padding like the arms of gigantic male dolls, thus Peter and I were walking across the pre-dawn snow, side by side. He was smoking his little curved white meerschaum pipe with the amber stem. The lines of elegance on his long face appeared to have been skillfully cut by a pointed instrument into Spanish leather.

"Yes," he said, "I accept your proposal. Ursula and I will welcome the regularity."

A single compact bird flew low over our heads and away in a long curving trajectory of great speed. Peter's breath was like snow that had undergone sudden transformation, the little round white bowl of his pipe reminded me of the gonad of some child god, a second bird skimmed by in pursuit of the first. And still he and I walked on together, contemplating the closeness achieved by certain psychic ties.

It was then, after we had walked perhaps another hundred yards, that I had my vision of Peter sealed at last in his lead box but with his penis bursting through the roof of the box like an angry asphodel.

⌘

On my way to the pool, which was small but deep and constructed in the shape of a slippery amoeba, I steadied myself against the pitch and roll of the bone-colored wooden deck and glanced up toward the projecting wing of the ship's bridge, where I saw him, hatless, black hair curling in the bright wind, arms on the rail, foot raised and resting on the white rung, tunic unbuttoned at the throat, bitter young eyes directed toward some invisible point off the prow of the ship, the kind of young wireless operator who would one day soon deserve the severest sentence of some maritime tribunal. I wondered what pocket in his tunic, left or right, contained one of the famous photographs. Clearly he was enjoying himself and not on duty.

But we dipped into another trough, the ship rolled to recover, the spray climbed high, I stumbled on toward the blue water gyrating now in the pool at the stern.

I staggered and dropped my book. The spray was sliding down the dark lenses of my sunglasses, today there could be no doubt of our motion and our direction. I was willing to suffer any amount of motion sickness, which

31

actually I did not anticipate at the moment, for the sake of just such comprehensible turbulence under a clear sun. I had only to balance myself at the edge of the pool, one hand on my belly and the other clutching the aluminum upright of the diving board, in order to perceive the reassuring concreteness of waves, foam, spray, persistent escort of gray gulls, a few orange rinds brightening our wake, the sudden dangerous angle of the bright blue water in the ship's pool. Our propellers, great pieces of underwater brass statuary, were today functioning with purpose, with power. There was no one in sight. I swayed, lifted my protected eyes toward the nearest gull, and then I felt the pool water —blue only because the inside of the pool itself was painted blue—rising and rolling upward to meet the flying spray.

"Allert," she called, precisely as my extended hands and head and puffy shoulders struck the blue water and I, with lungs distended and eyes open, began to descend. I took the small and feminine sound of her voice with me on my way to the bottom. As I dove down, a huge man in blue trunks upended in a small deep body of water that was pitching and sliding in counter-violence to the afternoon's heavy seas, the faint clear welcome voice remained afloat in my ear, like a second swimmer undulating downward with violent strokes. My name was submerged in the sound of her voice, her voice in my name, while I myself was deeply submerged in the pool of captive sea water that was thoroughly still now and of a darker blue than before. My eyes were open and I was working my arms and pectoral muscles in the slow rhythm of some luminous underwater butterfly. The nearest wall of the pool was driven into the water like a blue knife at a steep angle. A ladder-like series of empty holes for the hands and feet climbed sharply to the surface on which the shadows of spray and foam and the girl's outstretched leg were falling. I knew I was quite alone in the pool.

The invigorating pain of held breath, the black and white tiles like those of a lavatory floor, a drain hole covered with wire mesh, body more sensitive than ever to the weight of the water and the exertion of flotation, suddenly I had in fact achieved the bottom, as I was not always able to do on such occasions, and I put the flat of one hand on the tiles, concentrated on remaining down there as if anchored by a chunk of rusted iron, waited until I had surely propitiated the god of all those in fear of drowning at sea, and then pushed off, rolling onto my back, and prolonged the ritualized agony of the return to the surface by forcing my stiffened body to rise of its own accord, unaided by the use of either stroking hands or kicking feet.

"Allert," she called only moments after I re-emerged head and shoulders into the random forces of that bright day, "it's dangerous to swim when the sea is so rough!"

With a laugh and one upraised slippery arm I acknowledged her concern for my welfare and also conveyed my appreciation of her presence at the edge of the pool where she sat in splendid girlish near-nudity with one childish leg thrust over the water and dripping. I waved again, I snorted, I shook off the water, my shoulders heaved, I struck out to cover the short choppy distance to the glare of the fiery ladder. Gasping repeatedly and vora-

33

ciously for breath, and feeling the dead flow of all my returning weight, and managing to catch hold of the hot aluminum that was curled like the horns of some great artificial
goat, slowly I dragged myself back to the deck of the pitching ship and to the heat of the white towel which, while I
was on the bottom of the pool, she had spread out behind
her.

"Allert," she said as I collapsed face down on the
towel, "I am not going into the pool today. It's too rough.
I am not as strong as you are."

I grunted and rested my cheek on my soft pinkish
hands, one of which was pillowing the other, and felt the
upper portion of the small seated buttocks fitting tightly
into my hollow side while the water trickled slowly from
my ears and mouth. I did not need to open my eyes to
know she was there, since I could see her with my eyes
quite shut: scant and pale blue halter and bikini bottom
indistinguishable from underwear, small nubile body hairless and unmarked except for a scar in the shape of a fishhook below her navel, small face whose weight and shape
I could contain nicely in one hand, soft intensely black
hair concealed now beneath her bathing cap, little white
rubber bathing cap with the flaps upraised like those of a
pilot's old-fashioned leather helmet after an arduous flight.
Even with the warm water trickling from one of my ears
and the pain subsiding from my lungs and the ship pitching and rolling in a ring of bright spray, still in the darkness
I could see her perfectly because, as I had long since decided, she was the only other person on the ship I was
willing to know.

34

"Allert," she said more softly, though we were alone on the stern of the rising and falling ship and alone in the wind and sun, "how does it happen that you are such a smooth lover?"

"You seem to be speaking about oil," I replied, humming and mouthing the words with pleasure, "and not at all speaking about a man. Shame on you!"

But of course she responded at once to the kindly tone of my chiding by leaning down and placing her lips against the loose fat along my left shoulder and suddenly creating with her mouth, as small as it was, a sensation of extreme and pointed suction. Then she rested her cheek where her mouth had been and sighed, stretched out beside me and began gently stroking me in the rolls of fat along my ribs. Her cheek on my shoulder was like a wafer in a field of snow.

"Allert," she whispered, as we lay there under a curving sheet of bright spray, "let's go down to my cabin right now and strip off our clothes. Shall we?"

⌘

Her name, as I learned inevitably and fairly soon in the voyage, was Ariane. I thought that the name Ariane was quite typical of those elegant names bestowed so often on female children in poor families. At once I recognized the name for the type it was, and recognized its purpose, its poor taste, its pathos. At once I found the name extremely appealing because of its simplicity and sentimentality.

Ariane was the name of the young woman I knew so

emotionally and so briefly on the cruise. I do not find the name appealing now.

⌘

"Allert," Peter said, "I have a request. I would like to give you and Ursula an in-depth psychological test. Ursula agrees. And, after all, there is no reason why our friendship should not further my line of work. You must admit that the two of you would be excellent subjects. What do you say?"

He was smoking his pipe. I was smoking my cigar. Peter's darkened study smelled as if everything in it was constructed not of wood and leather, which was actually the case, but of compressed blocks of rich and acrid tobacco. Green tobacco, I thought, searching for my friend's profile in the unlighted room, remarkable green tobacco evocative of the time when I myself was a helpless boy.

"You know what I think of psychiatrists," I said with the cigar not inches from my waiting lips. "But for you, my friend, anything. In the right company I have nothing to hide."

Unfortunately Peter was not able to administer the test before his death.

⌘

My life has always been uncensored, overexposed. Each event, each situation, each image stands before me like a piece of film blackened from overexposure to intense light. The figures within my photographic frames are slick but charred. In the middle of the dark wood I am a golden horse lying dead on its side across the path and rotting.

"Why do I have the impression that we two are the only people on board this ship?"

"Perhaps because you are not in general friendly, Allert."

"But I am remarkably friendly as you well know."

"Besides, you are certainly aware of the officers and crew. You are aware of them all the time."

"Perhaps after all these years I am jealous."

"Poor Allert, there is no need to be."

✻

Peter, who was lean and naked, bent his knees and clasped his ankles and arched his spine and drew himself into his favorite Yoga position. His lap formed a broad and angular receptacle bearing his genitals which, I noted, lay there like some kind of excreted pile of waste fired in a blazing kiln and then varnished.

"The one thing you ought to know, Peter," Ursula was saying, "is that Allert and I go very well together in bed. We always have."

Ursula's honesty was quite enough to shatter the glaze on Peter's genitals.

✻

My cheeks were burning from the wind and sun, my lungs were filled with the smell of the sea. It was dusk and I was returning from my newly discovered place of utter privacy, a position on the bow of the ship concealed by the wheels and plates of a great winch painted with thick and glistening black paint. I had watched the sun lowering in

37

the western quadrant, I had detected no clue of approaching land. Was I free or lost, exhilarated or merely flushed with grief? I did not know. I did not know what to make of myself or of all these elements, these details, this fresh but oddly traumatic moment of sunset, except to intuit that I was more youthful and yet closer to death than I had ever been. At least my feelings were mixed, to say the least, when I inserted the brass key in the lock of my cabin door. The porthole, which gave only onto the deck, was sealed.

I saw immediately the small photograph lying undisturbed on the flat leather surface of my locked and as yet unpacked valise. Each object was in itself quite ordinary, the valise, the photograph, though taken together, the one on top of the other, each diminished in some small way the reality of the other, or at least altered it. With my hand on the brass door handle, and my hair and figure still disheveled from the touch of the now vanished wind, standing in this way just inside my cabin and seeing the photograph on the valise which in its turn lay on its stand, it was then that a new dictum passed slowly through my mind to the effect that the smallest alteration in the world of physical objects produces the severest and most frightening transformation of reality. Compared with the sight of the photograph curling slightly at the edges and lying somewhat off-center in the field of golden leather—ordinary, improbable, inexplicable, ringed with invisible chains of unanswerable questions—actual vandalism of my silent cabin, had it in fact occurred, would have been nothing.

I sat on my bed, leaned forward, and took the edge of the aging photograph between my thumb and index finger.

38

I held it as one might hold the wings of a submissive butterfly. Slowly I brought the photograph within range of my unemotional scrutiny. The two small white figures, like fading maggots, were apparently devouring each other sexually with carnivorous joy. I brought the picture closer to my quiet eye and stared at the crack that ran like a bolt of lightning across the glazed emulsion of the much-handled print. After a few more moments of study, I made up my mind that this was a different photograph from the one produced surreptitiously by the wireless officer in the dining saloon, though I could not be sure. It seemed to me that the figures were smaller now and more suggestive of another century.

I decided against destroying the picture. I decided against searching immediately for the wireless operator and facing him down. Though it was true that the unexplained appearance of the old-fashioned photograph in my locked stateroom was somehow worse than receiving a poison-pen letter, nonetheless I decided not to return the picture to its owner. If the wireless operator was attempting to intimidate me through the photograph or tell me something about myself that I did not know, all for the purpose of preventing my friendship with the young woman in the blue halter, he would soon realize that I was more formidable than he had thought.

No sooner had I made my decision and slipped the photograph into my jacket pocket than I leaned forward on impulse and unstrapped my valise, unlocked it, opened it wide. And though the articles inside were unfamiliar and appeared not to be mine, as if Ursula had determined that

39

my transformation as a result of travel would be complete in every way, nonetheless I unpacked my valise at last and found an appropriate shelf or drawer for each of the articles I was so unaccustomed to see or touch. I felt as if I had violated the coffin of some unknown child. I stored the valise in the bottom of the closet, hooked open the cabin door with its brass hook, unscrewed the fat brass wing nuts of my single porthole and thrust it ajar, and then lay down on my unfamiliar bed to wait.

⌘

The photograph is still in my possession. It is the last and in some ways an accidental addition to my extensive pornographic collection, though I have kept the fact of its existence hidden from Ursula all this time. I chose not to submit that photograph as evidence at the prolonged and sickening ordeal of the trial.

⌘

"Mr. Vanderveenan," she called as I reached the top of the ladder and rose head and shoulders into the wind and glare of the uppermost deck, "won't you join me for a game of net ball? I can find no one at all to play with me."

She was wearing a blue halter, tight blue denim trousers, black dancing slippers, and her hair tied back in a knotted strip of orange velveteen. She was standing in the wind beside the high net and balancing in one hand a black leather ball six or eight inches in diameter. Her waist between the lower edge of the halter and the upper edge of the leather-belted blue pants was bare. I recognized that her costume was the standard one generally intended to cause the viewer to imagine the belt unbuckled and the pants unzippered and hanging loose and partly open from the hips, and yet the naked waist was as smooth and child-like as the expression on her guileless face.

"I would like very much to play your net ball," I said into the invisible wind. "But tell me, how did you know my name?"

We were close together and partially concealed by the two pale blue smokestacks that were oval in cross section and leaning back at a wind-swept rakish angle in the thrust of our journey. The ball in her hand was a tight ripe sectioned fruit of black leather.

"The purser, of course. Didn't you know that he's one of the officers at our table? He knows the names and faces of all the passengers on the cruise."

"I see. The purser. Apparently I have not been aware of him."

We were closer together and I was quite familiar with the implications of the belted pants, the lure of the naked midriff. It was a commonplace attire. So far she promised nothing that was not in fact commonplace, except that her nearest shoulder blade was bare and poignant and that the miniature features of her face were grouped together in distinctive harmony. Even if she was an adult instead of a child and was a person who had actually lived beyond her majority, as I assumed she had, still she could never have come even close to half my age, a notion that engaged my attention occasionally from this moment on.

"You don't know the purser? Really? He's the one with the handlebar mustache. He's a favorite of mine."

"And who is the young officer who has assigned himself the seat next to mine at our table?"

"Oh, that's the wireless operator. He's another favorite of mine."

"You have many favorites."

She was smiling, I was closer than arm's length to her naked shoulder, I told myself that she could not possibly wish me to kiss her lips or even to touch her small bare shoulder so soon despite the inviting way she balanced the black ball, and despite her smile, her steady eyes, her upturned face. And yet I could in fact imagine this young person readily unbuckling her tight pants here in the space for games and athletics between smokestacks fore and aft and two white lifeboats on either side. And yet the poles of sex and friendship, I told myself, did not always imply the bright spark leaping between the two, at least not immediately.

"If you don't know the purser," she said, glancing down at the black leather ball, "then you don't know that my name is Ariane."

I reached for the ball, I felt the heat from the nearest smokestack mingling with the chill of the invisible wind and the bright light of the sun. Far below us a steward was moving along the hidden deck playing the three impersonal notes of his luncheon gong. The young woman's breathing was reflected in her bare navel as well as in the natural rhythm of the breasts supported only by the triangulation of the blue halter. Between her shoulder blades the halter was tied, I saw, in a crisp knot.

"So," I said, giving the ball a small toss, "so you are Ariane. It's a lovely name."

42

My tie was struggling in its clip, my hair was blowing, the dead white net was high above my head, I thought of the young woman's name and saw the brothers, the sisters, the anonymous girl in the luncheonette, the shabby baptism of the first-born and female child receiving the elevated name she would so often discover in cheap magazines in the offices of social welfare.

"Whatever you're thinking right now," she said, slipping her hand inside my jacket and her arm part way around my waist, "is unworthy of you. You shouldn't think such things, Mr. Vanderveenan."

"But your name is indeed lovely. You must remember that I mean what I say—always."

Her arm was around my waist, the slightness of her entire body was brushing against all the bulk of mine, I could feel her small ringless hand playing with the folds of my damp shirt in the area of the small of my back. Had anyone discovered us standing there together between the smokestacks, he would not have been able to detect her arm and hand concealed inside the formal drapery of my unbuttoned jacket. But I could feel the slight pressure on my waist, the faint tugging and stroking motions of the fingers of her left hand, by leaning down was able even to catch a smell of her breath which was fleeting and natural in the context of the ocean wind. Her gesture was a surprise of course, and for an instant caused me to experience another one of those rare pangs of anxiety and anticipation in the face of the first hint of sudden attraction. I thought she was being friendly, I thought that her physical gesture expressed warmth and playfulness without intention. And yet we were indeed leaning together on the uppermost deck

43

and one of her fingers had become somehow lodged between my belted trousers and my damp shirt. Already her entire manner should have told me plainly enough about her firmness of mind and her directness.

"Well," she said, raising her face toward mine and smiling, "you can't play net ball in your jacket."

"Just so," I said and drew my body away from hers, gave her the ball, removed my jacket, turned and walked into playing position on the other side of the net. The steadiness of the ship, the syllables murmuring in the wires overhead, the honed whiteness of the wooden deck, the symmetrical web of the high net, the sound of a ventilating machine, the wind at my back and the sun directly overhead so that time and direction were obliterated, these circumstances could not have been more concrete, more neutral, more devoid of meaning, more appropriate to the surprise and simplicity of the occasion at hand, when an unknown young woman was offering me something beyond innocence, companionship, flirtation. She was watching me as closely as I was watching her, and in both hands had raised the ball to chest level.

"You're traveling alone," she called, while I waited, raised my own hands in anticipation of her girlish throw.

"And you," I called back, squinting and waiting for the game to commence, "you too are traveling alone."

"But I'm different. I'm not married."

"Well," I called, laughing and wondering what had become of the desperate gulls, "I am married and I am nonetheless alone on this cruise. There's no more to say."

She raised the ball above her head. I took a step backward, I cupped my hands in the shape of the suspended ball. The ship was carrying us not toward any place but away.

"Often I go on these cruises," she called. "Often."

"Excellent," I called back. "Are you going to throw?"

She waited, this small anonymous female figure in an athletic pose. And then staring at me through the remarkable vibrations of the taut white net, slowly she lowered her arms until the ball, still gripped in her two hands, came to rest in the upper triangulation of her thighs, which were slightly spread. Her halter and tight pants appeared untouched by the wind, while on my back and shoulders and heavy legs my shirt and trousers were flattening like sails.

"I don't think so," she called without moving. "I think not."

I understood. Suddenly I began to understand the absolute presence of the girl who was waiting on the other side of the net and whose name was periodically carried on the passenger lists of ships such as ours. So I nodded and ducked under the net; she dropped the ball which, moving in accordance with the wind and slope of the deck, drifted under one of the lifeboats and disappeared over the starboard side of the ship.

We embraced. The skin of her naked back and shoulders was as smooth and glossy as the skin that has replaced burned skin on a human body. Her kissing was wet and confident, prolonged and wordless, and included even my nose, which she sucked into her small entirely serious mouth.

45

"You must never pity me," she said when we were
ready once more to descend the ladder. "That's what I
ask."

⌘

How could I possibly have done harm to such a person?

⌘

"Allert," Ursula was saying, "my reason for leaving
you is not sexual. Not at all sexual. It's just that you don't
know yourself, that you have no idea of what you are, that
in my opinion you are an open cesspool. Your jowls, your
eyes like lenses for the treatment of myopia, your little
cigars, your ungainly person, your perverse sense of humor,
all this is nothing to me. But you have long since emotionally annihilated yourself, Allert, and I can no longer toler-
ate your silences, your silence in the throes of passion, the
accounts of your dreams, the stink from the cesspool that
is yourself."

During this monologue a large white perfectly smooth
ceramic bowl filled with fresh fat purple grapes stood coolly
dripping on the table between us, which to me was either
especially thoughtless of Ursula or especially cruel.

⌘

The knuckles of the vibraphone player were round and
white and minutely smeared with small wet stains of fresh
blood. He was playing the metal bars of his silly instrument
with his knuckles which were split and bleeding. The bars

46

of the instrument were greased with the musician's blood. The drummer and the saxophone player were women.

✳

In my dream the nighttime village, which is poor and not at all the village of my birth, consists of no more than a dusty road flanked on one side by a candle-lit cathedral and on the other by a small unoccupied petrol station. The road is blanketed with dust and emerges from the darkness, the pitch darkness of empty night, into the brief space illuminated by the flickering light of the enormous anomaly of the cathedral—gothic, candle-lit in every crevice within and without, active with the breath of spirits, but empty— and illuminated also by the single unshaded bulb that glows beside the single outdoor pump of the petrol station. The road emerges into the light of the opposition between the palace for dead men and the hovel for dead autos, then disappears again into the night which to me is oddly familiar. I am not surprised to be alone in the barbaric village in this illuminated space within the context of the familiar night. I perceive and yet do not perceive the monstrous incongruity between the empty cathedral and abandoned petrol station, which consists of the pump and a doorless whitewashed hovel smelling of urine. Nor am I surprised at the silent appearance of the funeral procession, nor surprised to find myself a part of that procession as it too emerges into the light, a procession unattended by any person except myself and bearing in its slow midst only a high humpbacked black coffin. Nor surprised finally to discover myself identified with the coffin, as if it is my own

47

body that lies dressed for death inside. But when the coffin turns away into the great flickering panorama of the waiting cathedral, I turn in the opposite direction and pass through the unlighted and doorless entrance of the petrol station.

When I told this dream to Ursula, saying that it was one of my more important dreams, she laughed and said that I had not yet run out of gas, as she put it, despite my obvious fears. She picked up her magazine and remarked that I was actually fortunate not to have made my way already into the cathedral of death, reminding me of that other man who had died not so long ago and no matter how foolishly for her. Then she added that apparently I had not yet gotten over the religious hopes of my childhood after all, which was unfortunate since until I did those hopes would always be a screen between myself and the world in which I existed.

For some reason I chose that moment to ask Ursula if she ever discussed my dreams with Peter, but she did not reply.

⌘

"If you manage to destroy your guilt, my friend," Peter said, "you will destroy yourself. You are quite different from Ursula and even from me, for instance, since all your generosity and even your strength depend on unfathomable guilt, which is part of your charm."

While he stood there with pipe in mouth and the sun greasing the dead ducks at his feet, I told him in good-natured tones that I thought he was wrong.

"We'll see, my friend," he said. "We'll see."

In my dream I have become once more the silent little boy of my childhood, a plump and rather long-faced child in whom the features and temperament of the man to be are already evident, and I am securely situated in the village of my birth and, though it is clearly the darkest time of night and the village sleeps, nonetheless I am seated bibbed and powdered under a brightly shining light in the shop of the village barber. I hear running water, I hear the clicking of the shears, because the barber is wide-awake and at work on me. He smells of spice, and some kind of unguent that makes me quiver in pleasure and apprehension. We are alone, I am wearing my short trousers, my hiking boots, my monogrammed shirt with the broad white flowing collar. And from toes to neck my body is tented in the voluminous white bib which the barber has draped about me gently and pinned at my neck. I am drowsy, but I am totally aware of the night, the darkened streets and houses beyond the barber shop, the single electric light that smells like tallow, the movements of the barber who is clicking his steel shears between the slopes of my skull and the growth that is my childishly unattractive ear. But most of all I am aware of the barber's mirror.

Within the mirror's soft transparency I see myself, my slow eyes, and the blades of the steel shears. But into one edge of the rose-colored strips of wood that frame the mirror the barber has thrust a very large black and white photograph of a smiling girl who wears no clothes. She is seated on what appears to be the flowered bank of a canal for barges, and she is sitting with her legs to one side and

49

a slender arm propping up her thin and tender torso. Her clothes are piled at her side and in the right-hand portion of the photograph is plainly visible a small boy who is holding his bicycle and staring down at the naked girl posing so naturally for her photograph. Whenever I allow myself to stare into the soft white world of the mirror, watching the puffs of powder rising from the barber's great fluffy brush with which he sweeps my tingling neck, I cannot help but stare also at the girl whose naked breasts are to me totally unfamiliar. I stare at the girl's breasts, I cannot understand how they protrude as they do, nipped apparently by the spring and swollen.

The mirror and the photograph are drawing closer, the light sways, the barber turns my chair professionally, or so I think, but with the result that my view of the photograph is even more vivid than before. And I am aware of the tightness of the pants around my thighs, the smell of tallow, the girl's nakedness, my breath that has become swallowed somewhere inside me, a terrible and delightful sensation as of a little finger stiffening inside my pants. The girl is watching, the girl understands what is happening while I do not and can only attempt to control my breath and prevent the barber from discovering what strange metamorphosis is occurring inside my tent. I am aware of the smell of alcohol, the scent of lilacs, in the picture the boy's face is pained while I see in the mirror that my own face is pained as well. I find that I am spreading my plump thighs in a stealth quite unknown to me and that I am grinning in the unbearable pain of my boyish joy. And then I notice that the shears have stopped, that

50

the light bulb no longer sways, that the barber's face is suddenly close to my naked ear.

"Touch your little penis," he whispers gently, "touch it with the tip of your finger, little boy."

I gasp, I blush, I wait, and then I do as he says. The girl is smiling at me in approval but the darkness inside my tent is soaking wet and between my legs a fierce pain lingers in the wake of the shock that was triggered by the tip of my finger and the whispering sounds of the barber's voice.

When I told this dream to Ursula she said that it was charming and that it well explained my collector's interest in pornography. And yet it would have been better for me, she said, had I been the boy with the bicycle and had there been no photographer to interrupt the child's encounter with the sun-bathing girl. But of course it was amusing, she went on to say, that apparently even the rich life of sexuality shared by the two of us was still not sufficient to make unnecessary the psychic siphoning, as she called it, evident in my nocturnal emissions. It was then that she commented laughingly that I was drenched in sex.

⌘

I heard the tapping on the door. I heard excited voices and the sound of feet moving quickly across the deck outside. I heard the sound of her voice calling softly through the louvers of my cabin door.

"Allert? Are you there? We are passing the island. Won't you come and look?"

I waited, stretched flat on the coverlet, and quite distinctly I felt some alteration in the position of our tonnage as it shifted in the deep sea, and could not prevent myself from hearing the hivelike excitement of those passengers who were gathering on the starboard rail. I could hear the wind in the straw hats, I could hear the bodies crowding each other at the mahogany rail.

"Allert? Will you answer? I know you're there."

I was of course thoroughly certain that she could not possibly know that I was lying tensely inside my cabin since I had taken care to draw the green curtain across my porthole. And yet the very ordinary sound of her voice as well as her faith in my whereabouts, prompted me to reply.

"It is only an island, after all," I said evenly. "It is not Atlantis."

"It's important, Allert. Open the door."

"Very well," I said then. "In a moment."

"If you don't hurry we shall be past it and then there will be nothing to see."

I swung myself up from the bed and buttoned my shirt, drew on my trousers, opened the door. The intense light of midday, the ungainly binoculars on a strap around her neck, the now louder sounds of the expectant passengers, it was all exactly as I knew it would be, concreteness rotating toward illusion. And in my doorway, or nearly in my doorway, she was smiling and resting one small gentle hand on the binoculars.

"And Allert," she said in the voice that only I could hear, "have you been sleeping?"

"No," I said, closing and locking the door behind me and taking hold of one of her frail but well-proportioned arms, "no, I have not been sleeping. I have been meditating. As a matter of fact, Ariane, I have been wondering exactly who you are."

"But, Allert, you know who I am."

"More important, perhaps, I have been wondering exactly who I am."

"But I know who you are, Allert. And that's enough."

"Perhaps you do," I said, gazing to sea and thinking that her declaration was somehow more than an assertion of innocence, "perhaps you do indeed know after all. But where did you get that man-sized pair of binoculars?"

"From one of my friends, of course. We'll use them for looking at the island."

"Of course. From one of your friends. But tell me," I said then, diverting us back to one of the subjects I had been considering in my cabin. "What is your age?"

"Twenty-six, Allert. And yours?"

"Oh, I am much too old to say," I replied in a thicker, more milky voice. "Much too old to say."

"As you will, Allert. I really don't care about your age."

"But then it's probably true that in matters of shipboard romance, at least, the greater the disparity between the ages the better."

"You're in a very difficult mood today. I wish you'd stop."

"In a moment," I said then, and squeezing the thin arm, "in another moment I'll growl at you in Dutch."

She laughed, we were walking in step together, she caused her little hip to fall against my big pillowed flank,

53

she laughed again. And yet it seemed to me that even so she was still not completely reassured.

At this moment we rounded the great glass front of the observation lounge and strode hand in hand into the windy open space of the forward deck where, precisely as I had envisioned the scene, the group of passengers was gathered birdlike at the starboard rail. I was interested to see that they were more bizarre and yet not so numerous as I had thought. In particular I noticed one man whose body was not unusually masculine but who was naked except for a pair of khaki-colored shorts and an enormous rouge-colored conical straw hat that went down to his shoulders. A woman, heavy set and bold, was holding a small wicker basket filled with fruit, as if preparing to drop it quickly over the side.

"Allert," Ariane whispered as we squeezed to the rail, "they're all looking at you. They're all jealous because your companion is so young and so attractive."

"Yes," I whispered back, "they cannot imagine what we do together, but they have ideas."

"Oh, Allert," she said then, suddenly putting her hand on top of mine, "surely the captain is going to crash into the island!"

For a moment it seemed even to me that what Ariane had said was true. Because the island, a dry, treeless and apparently heart-shaped knoll, was rising out of the sea directly off our starboard bow. Considering the various angles of vision between masts, cables, diminishing horizon, approaching island, and considering the vast expanse of totally open sea in which the ship and island were the

54

only two concrete points—one fixed, one free—and that the space between the two was disappearing as quickly as breath, given all these circumstances it did indeed appear true that the captain was subjecting us all to unnecessary risk by changing course and by aiming the prow of the ship directly toward the arid heart of volcanic land anchored so permanently in the deep sea. Then I recovered myself and realized that for the first time during the voyage I was out of sympathy with Ariane, who, after all, was quite as capable as I was of common sense.

"Look," I said brusquely, "anyone can see there will be no collision."

"But we are very close to the island, Allert. Very close."

"Close," I said then in a gentler tone, "but safe."

We veered to within perhaps a hundred meters or so of the island. The man in the rouge-colored hat cried out and in an instant trained on the burning island the telescope of his terrible motion-picture camera, a camera I had failed to see, cradled as it was against his eye inside the cone of his hat. Ariane and I stood quietly touching each other and sharing the black binoculars, in the process of which she allowed her fingers to slide unconsciously over my buttocks while I, in turn, wet the vulnerable spot behind her ear with the tip of my tongue.

"It's so barren," she whispered, "so beautifully barren."

"Yes. And notice how the goats apparently manage nonetheless to survive on an island without food."

"It's because they're unreal, Allert. That's why."

But the goats were real enough for me, and though

there did not appear to be a blade of grass or the slightest sign of fresh water on the island, still the community of goats stood ruffled and silhouetted atop the nearest hummock and stared at what to them must have been the specter of a white ship bearing down on their final garden. Through the binoculars I could see the spray crowning the tightly spiraled horns, could see how old and young alike crowded together haunch to haunch, horns among horns, posing in the certainty of survival in the midst of pure desolation. The animals were as still as rocks, though their horns were flashing and their coats of long hair were blowing and ruffling in the emptiness of the ocean wind.

"The goats are real enough," I said. "But they are a strange sight. Even a haunting sight, perhaps."

"Allert," she said then, as if she had failed to hear my observation, "let's not allow them to disappear so easily. Come, let's watch until there's nothing more of them to see."

But it was only too clear that she neither doubted nor required my acquiescence, since she had taken back the binoculars and was already making her way out of the crowd and toward the stern of the ship which appeared now to be coasting past the island at an ever-diminishing nautical speed. Ariane walked swiftly, then ran, then walked swiftly again until finally she stood at the last extremity of the slowly moving ship, motionless with the binoculars dwarfing her face and her hard shoulder braced against the slick white glistening surface of the ship's flagpole.

We were crossing the pointed tip of the island, the goats were fading, I was standing directly behind Ariane who was pressed against the rail and against the flagpole, her small bare shoulders hunched in the intensity of her gaze.

I squinted at the disappearing island. I respected Ariane's concentration and did not press the front of my body to the back of hers, but waited as she sighted across our wake toward the island blazing less and less brightly in the dark sea. The hair was blowing at the nape of her neck, the ends of her halter knot were blowing between the shoulder blades which my own two hands could have so easily cupped, concealed, shielded. However, it seemed to me that Ariane was elated but also desperate as she attempted to hold in view the brown earth and the remote and mournful goats, so that I did not press the front of my pants into the seat of hers, no matter how gently, or put my finger where the wind was stirring the fine hairs on her neck. At the stern where we were standing together but separated, it was impossible to hear the engines or any other sounds of the ship, because that was the area most engulfed by the crosscurrents of the wind, the singing of the dead wake, the thrashing of the great blades just below us and just beneath the frothing chaos of the surface.

"Well," I said at last, "I'm glad you roused me for this event. It was an interesting sight. The abandoned goats, an island as bare as that one."

Slowly, as if once more she had failed to hear me, or as if she could not admit that now there was nothing to see except the empty sky, the unbearable sunlight, the gunmetal gray reaches of the ocean that was both flat and tossing, slowly she turned around and revealed her face from behind the disfigurement of the black binoculars, and leaned back against the rail, looked up at me, smiled, spread her legs somewhat apart. Her expression was open, clear, inviting. I noted how dark her skin had become since the start of the journey.

"But Allert," she said then, and her eyes were large, her teeth white, "the island we just passed belongs to me. Didn't you know?"

"Do you wish to explain yourself?"

"I do. Yes, I do. But another time."

Together we leaned on the rail and side by side stared at what we were leaving in our wake, which was nothing. But had I understood her meaning at that moment I would have bruised her in the agony of my desperate embrace.

⌘

The water comes down the surface of the glass, melting all vision. The water is an invisibly moving veneer of light on the black shale. The water is rearranging the pebbles that are so firm and white that they appear edible. The cold water spouts from the cleft in the rock, fills the tumbler, produces liquid weight in the earthen jar, emerges in cold bubbles from the bed of clay, sucks and gurgles through the moss, flows and drips and collects in the trees, the stream, the tall glass in my hand. And I drink it as I would breathe, letting it fill my oral cavity as it might a pool in the rocks, or I suck its freezing clarity against my teeth so that teeth and forehead ache with the cold. Or I hold it in the heavy pouch of my mouth and gulp it down, feel the clear cold water delivering itself to me drop by drop or in a steady transparent curve from silver spigot, brass tap, clay orifice with milky lips, and from the depths of frozen black trees. I wait, I drink, I consume the cold water beyond my usual capacity, making of myself a spongy reservoir, and teeth and gums and tongue and palate ache from the painful joy of this natural anesthetic. I feel that a spike has been driven into the back of my throat, my mouth is filled with the taste of white rocks and green ferns, I watch two large drops conforming to the laws of physics down the inside vertical space of the glass. And then I strike the match, grip the antithetical cigar between my front teeth, complete the cigar-lighting ritual—puffing, working the flame in slow wheels of light—and then at last the whitened tissues of my rinsed and empty mouth are bathed in smoke, are bathed and flooded with the thick gray smoke that tastes stronger than ever, more than ever like rich manure dug in bright golden gobs from a deep bed. That foul but cherished smoke is to the vanished water as Caliban was to Ariel, both of whom existed but in the mind.

⌘

Sometimes I hear myself saying *Ja-Ja-Ja* quickly, silently, so as to put a little spunk—to use Ursula's word—into my ponderousness. *Ja-Ja-Ja* I say to myself, and not even in Dutch.

⌘

"Allert," she said, "I do not mind your girl friends. I do not mind their visits in our household. I do not mind when one of them spends a few hours or the night sharing with

59

you the pleasures of the guest room bed. That's all very well. In a way it's enjoyable even for me. But I tell you, Allert, I refuse to have your friend Simone sitting on my handbag. How on earth could you fail to see? How could you fail to feel my mortification, my anger, and fail to pull her off by one of her innocent arms? I tell you, when I saw that woman sitting so ignorantly on all the intimacies of my own handbag, like a stupid chicken giving anal birth to my own uterine baggage, I tell you I began to question your judgment, your taste, even your motivations. I simply cannot have any woman putting her buttocks on my handbag. That she used her buttocks that way unconsciously is only the more insulting. So I trust we agree, Allert—no more Simone."

While hearing out this monologue I found that I was generally in agreement with Ursula, since I had indeed noted the episode in question but had reacted to its symbolic message with inward pleasure and amusement, rather than with Ursula's rage, for which I felt a certain additional shame while listening. But on the other hand, why did she have no sense of humor? And why did she leave her soft smooth leather handbag lying in the broad hollow of one of the sofa cushions precisely where poor Simone might be drawn unwittingly and might settle down upon it like some gentle victim on a land mine?

It was a trivial episode. And yet I was careful thereafter to make no jokes about Ursula's handbag, while poor Simone never again lay naked and bathed in candlelight on our guest room bed.

❖

Ursula was to me one woman and every woman. I was more than forty years old when we married, quite experienced enough to realize early in our relationship that Ursula was practical, physical, mythical, and that all the multiplicities of her natural power were not merely products of my own projections or even of the culture into which she was born—like a muted wind, a fist through glass—but to start with were engendered most explicitly in her name alone. Uterine, ugly, odorous, earthen, vulval, convolvulaceous, saline, mutable, seductive—the words, the qualities kept issuing without cessation from the round and beautiful sound of her name like bees from a hive or little fish from a tube. She has always been one woman and every woman to me because her attitudes have never been predictable, while minute by minute throughout the long years of our marriage her physical qualities have undergone constant metamorphosis from fat to lean, soft to hard, smooth to rough, lean to fat—languid urgent Ursula, who is leaving me.

✖

"Allert," she said, while masking her face with the smooth nightly glaze of thick white cream, "tell me the truth. Did you push her through the porthole as they accused you of doing?"

I could not bear the question. I could not believe the question. I could not answer the question. I could not believe that my wife could ever ask me that question. I could not bring myself to answer that question.

For me Ursula's eyes continued their lively movement

inside the holes in the white mask and in the darkness until long after she had returned for another one of her dreamless nights.

⌘

Together Ursula and I attended the funeral of the man who, not so long ago, shot himself in the mouth for her. Which makes me think that were he living, Peter might well be driving Ursula's car when she leaves. But he is not. Somewhere I have preserved the note written to Ursula by the man who allowed her life to prompt him into becoming a successful suicide. At least Peter knew better than to shoot himself in the mouth for Ursula.

⌘

"Allert," she asked me once, "how can you tell the difference between your life and your dreams? It seems to me that they are identical."

⌘

"Mr. Vanderveenan," she said, "will you come to my cabin for a moment? I have something to show you."

At the edge of the pool and in utter privacy she straddled the upper diving board like a child at play while I lounged upright and draped in my towel against the ladder. She had mounted to the upper diving board and now sat straddling the board backward so that I, holding the aluminum rail and she, hunching and leaning down with her hands braced forward between her spread wet thighs, were able to look at each other and to speak to each other as we wished. How long we had posed together in this tableau I could not have said, though at the sound of her invitation I felt on the one hand that we had never existed except together and in our tableau of mutual anticipation, but on the other that we had only moments before arrived at the pool's edge and that she had still to dive and I had still to help her dripping and laughing from the pool.

"By all means," I said, squinting up through the cocoa-colored lenses of my dark glasses, "let's go to your cabin."

She descended. I lifted her from the ladder. Hastily we used our towels, silently we collected our straw slippers, our books, our towels, our lotions, our straw hats for the sun. Her skin was brushed with lightlike pollen, I decided that the two little flesh-colored latex garments in which she swam had come from a cheap and crowded department store. The energy of her preparations, doffing the rubber cap and so forth, caused me to hurry.

"Not now, Mr. Larzar," she called to a broad-shouldered man dressed like the rest of the ship's officers in the somehow disreputable white uniform, and waving, "I have an engagement with Mr. Vanderveenan." And then, to me: "He wants his trousers pressed."

"But you are joking," I said as we descended to the dark corridor, "only joking."

"Whenever I am on a cruise I press the trousers of the ship's officers. I am not joking at all."

"I see," I answered. "But at least I would not want you to press my trousers."

"But of course you are not one of the ship's officers," she said in the darkness of the corridor below and laughed,

63

shifted the things in her arms, unhooked the brass hook, stood aside so as to allow me to enter first, then closed the door.

Blue jeans flung on the bed in the attitude of some invisible female wearer suffering rape, underclothes ravaged from an invisible clothesline and flung about the room, a second two-piece bathing costume exactly like the first but hanging from one of the ringbolts loose and protruding from the porthole, and cosmetics and pieces of crumpled tissue and a single stocking that might have fit the small shape of her naked leg, and magazines and sheets of writing paper and mismatched pieces of underclothing—in a glance I saw that the context in which her personal trimness nested, so to speak, was extreme girlish chaos of which she herself was apparently unaware.

"You may sit on the bed," she said, noting the antique typewriter in the upholstered chair, and without hesitation dropping towel and robe and slippers and so forth into the plump impersonal chair with the old machine. "Just clear a place for yourself. It doesn't matter if you're a little wet. Do you like my cabin? Is it as nice as yours?"

"Tell me," I said then, deliberately and gently, "why are we here?"

"I'll show you," she said, kneeling on the unmade bed where I was propped, "but I like this cabin because the porthole opens directly in the side of the ship. Whenever I wish to, I simply kneel on my bed and lean in my open porthole and smell the night or watch the sunlight in the waves. Do you see?"

While talking she had knelt on a pillow and pushed

64

wide open the porthole and now was leaning out head and shoulders with sunlight falling on her little narrow back and tension concentrated in her nearly naked buttocks made firm by the bending of her legs.

"That's a very agreeable demonstration," I said, "but for me it produces a certain anxiety."

"Why is that?" she asked, drawing in her head from the wind, the spray, "are you afraid I'll fall?"

"You are not very large, whereas in comparison to you the porthole is big and round. So I do not like you to lean out of it. My feelings are simple."

She knelt beside me, she studied my eyes, with both hands she better situated one of her small breasts in the little flesh-colored latex halter, the sun was a bright ball of light on the opposite wall.

"Mr. Vanderveenan," she said, "you are an old maid. I would not have believed it."

"I am not a man generally teased by women," I said slowly, filling the sentence with the white cadences of my native speech, and extending my hand which for a moment she lightly held, "and I do not enjoy the prospect of open portholes."

She was sitting on her heels, her knees were spread, I could see the outline of a label sewn inside her bikini pants as well as a little pubic darkness protruding like natural lace at the edges of the crotch. The sensation of her two hands on my extended hand was light and natural.

"Very well," she said, "I don't wish to cause you anxiety."

She smiled, I noted just below her navel a small scar

in the nasty shape of a fishhook, for a moment she raised my hand and touched it with her two dry lips. And then she drew back from me, got off the bed, rummaged about in an open drawer from which whole fistfuls of cheap underthings had already been half pulled, as if by some aggressive fetishist, until she found what she wanted and rose from where she had squatted, displaying to best advantage the roundness and symmetry of her little backside, and returned to me with the battered oblong case clutched to her chest. I rolled up from my slouching position. I sat on the edge of the bed. She sat beside me with the case on her knees and her shining skin smelling of talcum powder.

"So," I said as she opened the case, "so you play the flute."

She nodded, she smiled into the case at the sections of the silver instrument tarnished, I saw, with the myriad sentimental stains of a poor childhood focused at least in part on music. Then slowly and expertly she began to fit together the sections of the aged instrument which already reminded me of a silver snake suffering paralysis. It could not have been more clear to me that the poverty of her childhood had been forced to make way, finally, for the flute, as if the musical instrument, like a fancy name, would prove to be one of the avenues away from broken fences and a poor home. It was typical, it seemed to me, and the assembled anomalous instrument was proportionately much longer than I had thought.

"But this is a surprise," I said. "I did not know you were musical. Did you learn as a child?"

She nodded, she tapped the little metallic keys, she

66

arranged her arms and elbows in the contorted position all flutists assume when they commence to play. She tested the broad silver lip of the flute against her own small lip that was smooth and dry.

"I learned as a girl," she said, without lowering the old and battered flute from her childish mouth. "I was one of those fortunate schoolgirls to play in the local orchestra."

"And since that time," I said, and laughed, "you have continued to play your flute. It's a surprising accomplishment. It's quite wonderful."

"I think it is. And I want to play for you right now."

"By all means," I exclaimed, filling my words with whitewash and ducks and potato soup, "a little concert. Excellent, excellent."

"I know what you're thinking. But you'll see that my flute playing is not what you expect."

"Come, come, I'm listening," I said, laughing and attempting to strike the condescension from my heavy voice. "Let me hear what you can do with your flute."

"Very well," she answered then. "But it may not be as easy as you think. You see, I play in the nude."

And there in the little pathetic chaotic stateroom she did just that. With the door locked and the porthole wide to the menacing trident of the god of holidays, and standing within easy reach of my two clasped hands, slowly she removed her latex halter, stripped down the little latex bikini bottom, seated herself cross-legged on the end of the bed, picked up the instrument, puckered her lips, stared directly at me with soft eyes, and began to play. The first several notes moved me and surprised me even more than her nudity, since the notes were deep prolongd contralto notes, sustained with a throaty power and intention that suggested some mournful Pan rather than a small and ordinary young woman on a pleasure cruise.

"Forgive my banter," I whispered, allowing myself to slouch back again on the unmade bed and listen and to stare into the eyes of the naked flutist. "Your talent is serious."

From lonely little girl among stupid old men lewdly picking their strings and blowing their dented horns, from school orchestra composed of indifferent unskilled children, from days of practicing in an empty room smelling of beer and damp plaster, from all that to nudity and self-confidence and the ability to set into motion sinuous low notes loud enough and plaintive enough to calm the waves. And I had expected none of it, none of it. So I lay there propped on a heavy elbow. I was sexually aroused in the depths of my damp swimming trunks as I had not been since long before the disappearance of the ship's home port, and yet at the same time I was thoroughly absorbed in the shocking contralto sounds and the body bared as if for the music itself. I listened, I heard the reedy undulations, I noted the hair like a little dense furry tongue in the fork of her canted thighs, I saw the flickering of the little pallid scar and realized that she was taking no breaths, that the sound of the flute was continuous.

"Please," I said in a low voice, and momentarily allowing my free hand to cup the mound of my sex, "please do not stop."

Her mouth was wet, her eyes were on mine constantly,

except when occasionally she glanced out of the porthole or at the heavy helpless grip of my hand that was now the fulcrum on which I was minutely rocking, though still on my side. And throughout this improbable experience, simultaneously gift and ordeal, she was apparently unaware of the incongruity of all she was giving me behind the locked and louvered door.

And then in mid-phrase she stopped. She removed the flute several inches from her small chafed reddened mouth. Wet armpits, steady eyes, no smile, small breasts never exactly motionless, old flute held calmly in a horizontal silver line, the song quite gone, thus she abruptly stopped her performance and spoke to me as if nothing at all had happened.

"I'd like to relieve you now quickly," she said. "And will you spend the night here in my cabin?"

Then she moved, and in the silence of the disheveled cabin I could hear that all the low notes of the silver flute were still making their serpentine way beyond the porthole and in the transitory wastes of sea and sky.

※

I was standing in the bow with my feet apart, my hands gripping the wet iron, my collar open and tie loose, my shape defined by the steady pressure of the invisible wind. It was dawn, the sun was bright, my face was wet, the sharp prow was rising and falling steeply, slowly, as if in some slow-motion field of monstrous magnetism. I heard what sounded like a city of distant voices and smelled the faint smells of a landfall, though on the horizon there was no indication whatsoever of ship, shore, island, volcanic cone. Directly beneath my spread feet I felt the rumble of the anchor chain. I heard that terrible noise distinctly and felt the black chains descending link by mammoth link as if we were going to drop both anchors and remain forever in the midst of that natural desolation known only to birds.

But we continued to move up and down and forward in the dawn sea. I composed myself and took deep breaths. I thought of my young friend. And on we sailed.

❇

In the earlier stages of my voyage I contracted a rash. At first nothing more than a constellation of a few blemishes or pimples circling the navel, slowly it reproduced itself on the front of my belly until, months later, it had grown into a thick circular bed of inflammation surrounding the navel like a graft made from the livid flesh of ripe strawberries. No doubt my skin played host to the first spores while from beneath bare arms I watched the small figure of the young woman sitting alone at the pool. The first seed must have lodged in my eye. Or was the rash sexual in nature and intended to affect the organs of the loins, and had it somehow become displaced instead to my receptive belly? What began as a pimple or two has flowered into a large circular field with the navel as the undamaged hub. Soon it will become a constant and faintly breathing girdle of wet contagion.

❇

The two small naked figures were crawling and squirming in the palm of my hand. Though the photograph was in fact safely concealed in my jacket pocket, still the two white figures were clearly there, small and fiercely wriggling on the smooth glossy skin of the palm of my right hand, as if the pink living skin of my palm had become a little bed of photographic emulsion developed and hardened and translucent.

But when I reminded myself of the similar plight of Macbeth's poor queen, and then rubbed the offending palm against the fruit of my own genitalia, the little image of the old-fashioned naked lovers faded and fled completely away for once and for all.

⌘

Her cabin door was wide. She was at her ironing. Wearing only her frayed tight denim pants so that her feet and torso were quite bare, thus she stood with her back to me and her hair pinned up and her iron traveling down a crease in the white pants. I hardly paused but it was enough for me to see the finger marks down the length of her spine, the shadows moving at the edges of the little shoulder blades and in the nape of her neck, the red teeth marks where the elastic band of her underpants had been, the new skin of the upper buttocks shining against the tightness of the leather belt, the fleeting impression of one small naked breast flung partially into view in the exertion of her girlish labor. And my accidental passing was enough to reveal to me that the large and hairy shank of the man stretched out on her unmade bed and reading, waiting for the return of his trousers with his face concealed behind an open magazine and one brutal and hairy leg raised and bent at the knee, belonged not at all to the wireless operator as I had expected but instead to some other ship's officer newly favored with my young friend's generosity.

I forced myself to continue on to the ship's pool where immediately I dove to the bottom and competed for breath, for time, for anguish, for peace, with the other shadows I found lurking there.

⌘

In my dream the night is as pure and dark as a blackened negative, and yet I am well aware of the field at the edge of which I stand and of the chateau which is somehow silhouetted on the opposite side of the field, though the horizon itself is not visible. I stand there, realizing that nothing whatsoever exists in the world except the night, the stone chateau, the waiting field, myself. The chateau and field are thick with significance, though I have seen neither in my past life.

As I cross the field, taking slow careful steps but determined to reach the ominous yet familiar stone building at any cost, I become aware that the entire sloping field has been blanketed with enormous soft round pads of cow manure. They are round as flagstones, thick as the width of a man's hand on edge, spongy within and thickly encrusted without, soft and resilient and yet able to bear the full weight of a heavy man, though there is always the possibility of piercing the crust and sinking into the slime within. I am picking my way with care and yet also treading on the uncertain field with excitement because no one has ever crossed this field before. But suddenly I know that the shapes lying like dark and spongy land mines beneath my feet are composed not of cow dung, as I had thought, but of congealed blood. With awe and a certain elation I realize that I am walking across a field of blood. And I know too that though I am proceeding toward the chateau, I am also walking somehow backward in time.

I step carefully. I do not want to pierce the crusts and sink to my ankles in coagulated blood, and yet it is necessary to walk across the field, and I do so with pleasure as well as fear. The pads of blood have been arranged on the field's dark acreage with their edges touching, symmetrically, and to me they seem on the one hand fresh and moist and on the other old and long-ripened like cheese or manure.

Between the far edge of the field and the dark stone facing of the baronial hall there is a ditch. I am positive that the ditch is there and yet I fail to see it and spend no energy crossing it, though I am conscious that I have in fact passed beyond the empty ditch in the middle of the unchanging night.

I approach the cold chateau from the side, moving as if by perfect instinct not to the main gate but to another and smaller entrance in the thick side wall. I know where I am going, I am in possession of myself, and yet I know too that I have no history, no recollection of the past, so that my life, which is specific, depends only on the field, the ditch, the night, and what I am about to experience within the chateau. I know the way. There is nothing else.

The chateau is empty. I enter as if by plan, and I find that the great stone hall consists only of a single vast room that is empty, dusty, cold, from floor to roof windowless

73

and desolate except for one small structure standing altar-like and frightening in the center of the stone floor. I approach, I am breathing deeply. Erect and with hands at my sides I face the sacred structure which is twice my height and circular at the base and pointed on top—like some prehistoric tribal tent—and covered entirely with dry and hairless animal skins.

The skins are hard, scaly, wrinkled, and completely without hair. The light in the vast stone room is gray, the air is cold, the construction of dead skins is familiar and unfamiliar as well. Slowly and conscious only of myself as neutral and of the action as charged, slowly I descend to my knees, insert my fingers in the seam where two large bottom skins are joined, and slowly pull them apart until the darkness will accommodate my entry on all fours. So I, a man fully grown and yet also reduced to my simple and now curiously unemotional intention, on all fours work my way head and shoulders and hips and heavy legs inside the second structure where in a meaningless crouch I survey the desolation of my own beginning. The circular and conical space inside the dead skins contains nothing at all except a dusty floor and a small iron hearth partially heaped with ashes which are both dry and moist. The fire is gone, the ashes have stood so long that here and there they have become crystalline, I see a few bones and feathers embedded like Norse relics in the dead ashes. Now I realize that I had hoped for more, had expected more, and yet in the midst of such silence and immobility I also realize that my disappointment is nothing compared with the journey I have just taken and the barren actuality I have at last discovered.

74

When I reported this dream in meticulous detail to Ursula, insisting that it was central to my life, since few men are privileged and courageous enough to undertake this journey, her only reply was that it was obviously someone else's womb, not hers, that had become so inhospitable to my regressive drives. Her own womb, she answered me, was warm and receptive always, as I surely knew.

⌘

"But I disagree with your cesspool metaphor," I said, waiting for her to face me in the leather chair. "It's simply that I am in love with Psyche. I have always been in love with Psyche. And I happen to know that whenever I express the need I can trust my Psyche to send me up a fresh bucket of slime. Unlike you," I said, studying the level of water in my clear glass, "I am not afraid of Psyche's slime. I do not find it distasteful. As a matter of fact, without my periodic buckets, I could not survive. Now tell me," I said, feeling the cigar swimming toward my fingers through the semidarkness, "isn't my metaphor preferable to yours? It is truer, Ursula, more just, more compassionate."

⌘

"Allert," she said, "have you ever realized that you have the face of a fetus? The eyes, the jowls, the florid complexion are all deceiving. If you look closely enough you'll see, as I have just seen, that actually you have the face of a fetus. Perhaps that is why you dream rather than live your life."

⌘

In my dream it is nighttime on the grounds of Peter's hospital. My impression is that I have never seen this place before yet I know it well. Acres Wild, as it is called, extends without limit through the night, but also is carefully tended by capped and muffled gardeners and, sooner or later, stops at the perimeter of the high serpentine brick wall. All this I know somehow and even without letting the words come silently to mind. But now through the tall trees the rain is falling, in each of the small white cabins a single naked bulb is burning. And I am mobilized, I am worried, I have an urgent task requiring Peter's help.

"Peter," I say in the dream, "I must talk with you."

We are in the main building and Peter, wearing his white coat, is surrounded by a group of young men and women. My face and clothes are wet, he does not wish to give me his attention. The young men and women are too attractive, too interested in what he is telling them in his musical and confidential tones.

"Peter," I say, and at last he stares at me over the shoulder of a slender blonde young woman. "Why is she here? She has no business here. She is different from all the rest, she is quite special. If you don't help me, Peter, who knows what harm they may do her under the mistaken thought that she too is one of your patients?"

It is raining, my white shirt smells as if it has been sprinkled with the juice of clams, my feet are bare. And I am agitated over the problem of Ursula's welfare. But Peter removes a thick black professional fountain pen from the pocket of his long white coat and on a spongy paper napkin writes what I presume are instructions to those invisible

76

attendants who will either set Ursula free or do her harm.

I accept the instructions, I express my thanks, I see that Peter is returning the fat pen to the breast pocket of his long white coat. He appears quite unconcerned about Ursula or my own atypical need for haste. The voices of the young men and women are wet with admiration as if Peter is their celebrity as well as doctor. Instructions in hand I hurry again into the rain which has become a combination of white mist and dripping leaves.

The light in Ursula's cabin smells of tallow. The bulb is naked and yet casts an orange light over all the damp interior of that small screened-in white cabin into which Ursula is settling, making herself comfortable, as if the cabin were facing an empty beach instead of standing in the center of the grounds of Peter's hospital. Inside the cabin there is no one but Ursula, who is spreading a sheet, removing the contents of her valise, only unwary Ursula and no one to whom I might show Peter's lengthy hand-written instructions to send Ursula back to her home, her garden, her magazines, her husband. But even so, when I glance at the instructions I see that the paper napkin has absorbed the rain and that the ink has become hopelessly blurred.

"Don't you see where you are?" I say. "Don't you understand?"

But she only smiles and smooths the sheet, while I in anxiety and frustration take full note of the fact that the cabin is half garage, half cabin, so that the ambulance may enter the cabin itself and deposit the unruly patient directly into the waiting bed. And I also take full note of the thickly padded straps attached to the bed, the enamel pan beneath a cheap table, the smell of some terrible drug that lingers on the damp air.

The orange light, the smell of a burning candle, the smell of the drug, the padding on the bedstraps as thick as my arm, it is a stage setting with which I am familiar and unfamiliar both, and in which I am more afraid than ever.

"We must go," I whisper, "we must leave at once."

But Ursula only smiles, leaning over the bed, and draws up the sleeve of her simple yellow dress that has fallen away to expose some of the fullness of her perfect shoulder, and speaks. As long as Peter is there, she tells me, we have nothing to fear.

When I told this dream to Ursula she remarked that the drug in my dream was in all likelihood paraldehyde, which she remembered hearing about somewhere in the past. Then she walked across the room and stood looking down at me where I sat in the leather chair and said that never, never, would I be able to wrap her in the rubber sheet, as she expressed it, of my destructive unconscious and, further, that I should take this dream as a warning, not about the state of her psychic life but mine.

At that moment it occurred to me once again that Ursula was quite capable of preserving herself psychologically at my expense. Then I began to search myself for the reason she had used the metaphor of the rubber sheet.

✳

"Did you do it?" she asked, cupping the roses against her breasts. "Did you, Allert? Did you? I want to know."

The smell of the raw sea beneath the pier, between the ship and pier, and the smell of wood, of tar, of fresh paint, of petrol, of salt, of engine oil lapping the insides of vast steel drums, and the smell of perfume and distant schools of dead fish and of thick new lengths of hawser across the crowded pier like fresh nets for the unwary, in the midst of it all I felt as if I were wearing the rubber suit of the skin diver beneath my clothes. In the grip of the steam whistle my body was drowning in its own breath. Inside the rubber skin I was a person generating his own unwanted lubricant of poisoned grease. Even as Ursula propelled me toward the gangplank I felt myself sinking. For a moment I longed for a quick slice of the surgeon's knife as if I were my own ulcer and only the cold punctuating knife of the surgeon could bring relief.

"It's so exciting, Allert," she said on tiptoe with her lips to my ear, "don't you agree?"

✱

"Allert," she said, "I wish you'd stop poeticizing my crotch. It's only anatomy, after all. There's nothing mysterious about it. It could hardly be more familiar, to you at least."

"It is quite true," I murmured, feeling for the ash tray in the darkness, "that I am intimately aware of your anatomy. But you might as well try to persuade me that the conch shell, for instance, is not mysterious. You'll never convince me, Ursula. Never. The conch shell and its human anatomical analogue are mysteries. The imagination cannot be denied."

�֎

Hollander, beast of the dream, head of the household, suddenly I awoke and pushed myself upright among the pillows. The air was of neutral temperature and yet the cold night was inside the house, it seemed, so that the carpeting smelled of dead leaves while the darkness was fusing itself with the night stars. I was unconscious of sexual inclinations, I wanted only to see the snow outside. So I swung clear of the softness and heat of my enormous bed, found my robe and stood by one of the windows tying my robe. Below me the snow was a thin unviolated white crust spread as with a trowel between the house and the black edge of the naked trees in the distance. In the starlight and at the edge of the house the frosty rear end of Peter's car was barely visible. I took a deep breath, another, and through the years, the darkness, the coldness of this drifting night I caught for a moment the fleeting telltale scent of the flowers that once filled my childhood.

I pressed my cheek to the cold glass and decided to forgive Ursula for saying in Peter's presence that I had the face of a fetus.

Her door was closed. It was constructed of solid oak and closed with all the finality of unlighted houses, midnight rituals, silent rooms. But Ursula's bedroom door was unlocked, as I discovered as soon as my warm hand closed on the cold sphere of solid brass that was the knob. I myself could not hear the door knob turning, I myself could

not hear the sound of my breath or of my wrinkling robe
or of my bare feet on Ursula's white tufted rug. And yet
Ursula must have heard my slightest movement and the
tones of my very determination to make no noise, because
as soon as I entered that room and closed the door behind
me and approached her bed, which was thoroughly visible
thanks to the cold stars and the crust of reflecting snow,
she spoke to me, clearly but softly so as not to disturb
Peter who was asleep at her side.

"Allert," she said in the silver light, "what do you
want?"

Her voice was low, clear, soft, feline, neither charitable
nor uncharitable, neither kind nor cruel. In the midst of
the scented sheets, the pillows in their satin skins, the
peach-colored comforter filled with the fuzz of ducklings,
there she lay with her head turned in my direction and
Peter's jaw thrust against her left shoulder like the point
of a hook. Ursula's eyes were fixed on mine. Peter was
snoring.

"Go away, Allert," she said then, quietly, simply.
"Peter needs his sleep."

Peter's white pajamas on the floor, Ursula's short
transparent Roman toga at the foot of the bed, the heat of
the two nude bodies beneath the soft bedclothes drawn up
to their chests, the feeling of Ursula's eyes on mine and
the sight of Peter's neck and shoulder muscles that appeared shrunken and cast in sinuous silver, the moment
was so familiar, peaceful, even alluring, that I felt in no
way the intruder and took no offence at the harshness of
what Ursula was saying.

I removed my robe, I dropped my pajama trousers, I scrubbed the hair on my chest and around my nipples with stubby fingers.

"All right," she said, as I drew back the covers, as the snoring stopped, as she raised herself on one elbow, as I thought of Peter's automobile waiting below in the night's frost, "all right, we'll go to your room."

"No, Ursula," I said in return and sliding under the bedclothes like a ship in the dark and stretching out against the heat and smoothness of her naked length, "tonight I prefer your room, not mine."

She said nothing. The snoring recommenced. Gently I pushed away Peter's hand from where I encountered it on Ursula's belly that was tawny and filled with the morning sun, the evening cream.

"If you control yourself," I said in a low voice appropriate to lavish beds and nocturnal games, "he will not wake. Believe me."

"Allert," she whispered, "you are not amusing."

"But it is just as I suspected," I whispered, "you have never been readier. Never."

"But have you forgotten Peter?"

"Let Peter sleep."

"But it's impossible. It makes no sense."

"Except to me, Ursula, to me. And I want it so."

In the morning we sat together in the alcove and ate the goose eggs boiled by Ursula, who was still wearing only her Roman toga through which the morning sun shone as through the clear windowpanes. The morning light, the goblets of cold water, the cubes of butter sinking into the centers of each of the great white eggs with their untamed flavor and decapitated shells, and the aroma of coffee and the contrast between Ursula in her usual near-nudity and Peter and me in our plaid robes, the deep peace and clarity of the moment—all of it made me more securely aware than ever of the relationship between the coldness outside, where the geese were honking, and the warmth within.

"I see now, Allert," he said, lifting his clear glass, lifting his spoon, "that you too are capable of deception. It is not a pleasing thought, my friend. Not at all."

"But, Peter," I objected pleasantly, "you must not forget that I am the husband."

"Nor must you forget, my friend, that I am the lover."

"But Peter," Ursula said, interrupting us and thrusting a bare hand inside Peter's robe, "let's forgive Allert. I think we should."

"Of course we'll forgive him," Peter said, smiling and paying no attention to Ursula's hand, "in due time."

Beneath the table Ursula's bare foot was probing mine. In the sunlight Peter had the long thin face of a Spanish inquisitor.

✳

"The trouble with you, Allert," she said, pulling off her firebird bikini and standing thick and soft and naked on Peter's beach, "is that you think you're Casanova. What you do is one thing, what you think of yourself is another. And you think of yourself as Casanova. But all the *amours* in the world do not mean that you are attractive to women. Don't you see?"

But the idea, like so many of Ursula's ideas, was completely invalid. Never did I for a moment form such a self-image. Never did I think of myself pridefully. I am not interested in the long thread of golden hair hanging from the tower window.

✼

Naked and resting on all fours on the leather divan in the darkness, wrapped in her tawny nakedness as another woman might partially cover herself in the skin of a lion, and resting on her knees and elbows with her buttocks thrust high and glazed as with melted butter, thus she swayed and waited in the darkness for either Peter or me to rise and approach and take advantage of her position on the divan. In a low voice she was crooning an unmistakably serious invitation to Peter and me.

I was the first to move.

✼

When she leaves, when she is finally gone, when she terminates all the processes of leaving and disappears at last, in all this will there be some kind of gain for me? I anticipate no loss, no hours of stunned grief. But what of the possibility of gain? Ursula is leaving me deliberately. Ursula intends to spare herself my distasteful presence, to neutralize my acid with her departure. But Ursula also anticipates enrichment in the unknown life she plans to pursue. Will I also find enrichment when I am left alone? In emptiness will I discover freedom? Will I cry out once again for Simone? Will I write letters and make long-

84

distance telephone calls until at least a few of the women I have known in the past return to me? But more than likely I will write no letters, make no telephone calls, do nothing. More than likely I will leave the enrichment to Ursula. But whatever I do or however long I stand at the window, never again will I commit my life to marriage. On the subject of marriage I share completely Ursula's sultry vehemence. I am happy to admit our total agreement on the subject of the burning bridal gown, the cigar in the dark.

✶

When I again glanced down to the crowd on the pier, I saw that she was no longer waving but was swinging her handbag back and forth on its leather strap and staring up at me, where I stood at the rail, with a face that was merely fleshly and quite drained of expression. Then she was gone, as though that white ship would never again return to its home port. The baskets of flowers heaped on the deck reminded me of the banks of living flowers in a crematorium. The flames from the engine room glowed on the deck. The first blast of the whistle cut back and forth through my body like an invisible beam. We began to move.

✶

In the darkness and through the open porthole I smelled the scent of orange blossoms, the aroma of dead dust, the smell of lemons flickering on some distant hillside, even a few faint traces of eucalyptus oil floating just beyond the reach of the waves. But when I struggled into my trousers and went out on deck to investigate, exposing myself once more to the darkness and the wet night air, I realized that we were still two or three days from our next port of call. I stood at the rail only a moment, yet long enough to be discovered by Ariane and to arouse her fear. She emerged from the shadows, she hesitated, she approached, she clung to my arm.

"So you too have those feelings," she whispered. "I thought you did."

For answer I drew her abruptly into my dark stateroom, thrust her roughly down onto the disheveled bed and bruised her in the agony of my desperate embrace.

⌘

It was dusk when we glided out from among the trees and across the last white slope toward Peter's house in the country. I heard the sibilance of our skis on the snow, I smelled the resin on the cold air, I heard their laughter as Peter and Ursula made playful stabbing gestures at each other with their bamboo poles. The light of the first stars purled impossibly through the last light of the day, so that in the cold gray atmosphere there was a hint of pink. Ursula lost her balance, thrust out her rump, spread wide her skis, recovered. A single small bell tolled in some distant village where no doubt the cold sexton stood alone pulling the rope, and Peter made clacking noises with his skis on the snow.

"Well, Allert," Peter said, divesting himself of skis, mittens, ski poles and the bulky knitted sweater that portrayed two angular black deer on a field of white yarn, "it was a good way to spend an afternoon, don't you think?"

"I enjoyed myself," I said, recalling the playful shouts, the flat white hours, the black trees bleeding at the edge of our path. "Going cross-country with you is always a pleasure. Even Ursula becomes animated on these occasions. Is it not so, Ursula?"

She was smiling, our faces were florid, our boots were creaking, our skis were properly upright in the rack against the white wall of the house. We stamped off the snow, we laughed, we put our arms across each other's shoulders, Peter favored Ursula with a prolonged kiss. When they pulled apart, cold and at the same time tingling, the first few white flakes began to come down.

"So," I said, glancing into the approaching night, "to-morrow there will be no sign of where we have been today."

"That's an oddly mordant remark, my friend," Peter said. "Come, let's enjoy some black rum and a roaring fire."

"Peter's nice," Ursula said then, with nothing but internal whim to justify her indulgent non sequitur. "Isn't he nice, Allert?"

"A little old," I murmured, thinking of a white chateau, a dark field, a night of ice, "but an excellent friend."

"But Peter's in his prime, Allert. That's what I mean."

"Well, then, it sounds to me as if Peter deserves another one of your wet kisses."

"Exactly," Peter said then, squeezing Ursula's waist, "but in front of the fire. In front of the fire."

The animal skins were heaped before the hearth as usual and the fire was high. The jaws of the polar bear into which Ursula had flung a stein of beer one steaming night, the hide of the tiger that was worn and smooth like a map composed of dust and sand, the long dark silken hair of a water buffalo long dead and headless, there they lay, adorned as usual with small soft brightly colored pillows and the light of the fire. In the large room totally dark except for the fire, the skins and pillows were an island of sensuality in a cold sea, and as usual it was Ursula, rather than Peter or I, who became the waiting castaway on that floating island. She sank into the fur of the water buffalo, she yawned, on her stomach she propped her pelvis on the head of the bear, like a child she smiled into the light of the fire, she sat up in order to accept the thick glass from Peter.

"Schnapps for Allert, rum for you and me," she said. "But you forgot your wet kiss," she said, and drew Peter's mouth down to her own. And I, stretched out on the edge of the polar bear skin, took a few rapid sips from my glass and noted the rough texture of Peter's amber-colored corduroy pants and the roll of warm flesh between the waistband of Ursula's ski pants and the lower edge of her black turtleneck sweater. My stocking feet were crossed at the ankles, I wriggled my toes, I saw for a moment the little familiar plug of gold in Ursula's left incisor when Peter pulled his mouth away in a simulated playful need for breath.

"More schnapps, my friend? Please help yourself."

All around us the house was empty, filled with shadows and cold beds, drawn blinds, and from the dusty high-fidelity equipment in one of the darkened corners of the cold room in which we lay came the sound of half a dozen baroque recorders singing with the austerity of artificial birds. I heard the music, I tasted the cold night, I smelled the steam of our outdoor clothing and hairy socks. In the fireplace, which was extremely wide and constructed of stones hauled laboriously from a nearby field, the logs were as large as the bodies of young children and were burning as in the aftermath of some prehistoric fire. Ursula was smoking one of her infrequent cigarettes, the schnapps was strong. I heard Peter's footsteps in the hallway, above our heads, behind me, and then Peter returned to us and dumped the soft Nordic blanket between Ursula and me and placed the several plastic containers of body lotion on the hearth to warm.

"More schnapps, my friend? Please help yourself."

Gently Ursula freed herself from Peter's hand and stood up between us and pulled off her ski pants. Our clothes were steaming. The snow was banking up on the darkened windows, the sprawling fire was casting its hot patina on the skin of Ursula's bare legs between her woolen socks and the tightness of her scanty beige-colored trans-lucent underpants.

"Well," Ursula said, tossing her half-smoked cigarette to the waiting flames, "now you see what you have done with your rum and fire."

She turned and pushed up the sleeves of her knitted sweater. In the shadows the fat crotch of her elasticized underpants looked as if it had just been roughly cupped in the wet grip of an anxious hand. And smiling, pushing up her sleeves, patting her broad stomach beneath the sweater, down Ursula sank to her elbows and knees, lowering her face to the touch of the buffalo hair and raising her wide tight buttocks to the glow of the fire. She was contracting and loosening the small of her back, thrusting high her shining rump, stretching her fingers, smiling and rubbing her face to and fro on the buffalo hair.

"I don't know about you, my friend," Peter said in a low voice with his eyes on Ursula and his head tilted toward the sound of the recorders, "but I find this scene extremely attractive."

"And I too, Peter. But Ursula should be surrounded by golden tumbling cubs, should she not?"

"You are always jocular, my friend. Always so jocular when it comes to the life of the sexual being."

"It is true. You have your psychiatric patients, I have Ursula and my sense of humor."

"But Allert has never been possessive," Ursula said, filling our pause with the sound of her throaty words and the sight of her backside rotating closer and closer to the heat of the fire, "that at least can be said for him."

"Tell me," I said then, changing the subject and feeling Ursula's strong fingers picking tufts of hair from my right-hand sock, "what is your professional opinion on the inability to believe in the reality of the human self?"

"It is a familiar question. And a familiar condition as well."

"Sooner or later," I said, aware of Ursula's fingers and seeing Ursula's honey-colored eyes in the flickering shadows and noting the red silk pillow on which she was now propping her chin, "sooner or later the young child discovers that he cannot account for himself. As soon as he becomes inexplicable he becomes unreal. Immediately everything else becomes unreal as one might expect. The rest is puzzlement. Or terror."

Everything about our present condition—the cold house, the snow falling invisibly outside, the rugs and pillows and fire, the chorus of *blokfluiten* reminding me for some reason of the time when, as a child, I was taken on a trip to Breda—all of it was conducive to wandering ideas, to a slow and unmistakable drift toward sensuality. Peter was filling our glasses, his brow was aglow with perspiration, to me the musty animal smell of the old polar bear rug evoked images of faceless hunters stalking the ice floes in search of death. Ursula had abandoned my thick sock and was holding Peter's ankle in a tight grip. In the faintest possible rhythm her backside was undulating now in the greasy heat of the fire.

"So, Peter," I murmured, "you have no thoughts on my query?"

"If you insist, I can only say that you and I are too old for this conversation. Much too old."

"But it's quite true," Ursula said slowly, drowsily, "Allert is not real."

"On religious questions," Peter said, with his scarred face long and dark and composed in the light of the fire, "I am afraid I cannot be of any help. No help at all."

"But if I disagree with you," I said quietly, "and if you are wrong, and if the problem is not religious but is in fact psychological, what then?"

"Please, my friend. It is not like you to become aggressive."

"Allert aggressive! What a nice idea."

"Ursula," I murmured then, "perhaps you would like to take off your heavy sweater. For Peter and me."

"You'd have me bare-breasted, is that it?"

"Yes. Play with your nipples, Ursula. For Peter and me."

"You're trying to arouse me, Allert! But I'm sorry, you'll have to wait."

"Jocular, philosophical, impatient," Peter said. "What is the matter with you tonight, my friend?"

"Today on the skis," I murmured and closed my eyes, raised my head, "I felt pleasantly athletic. But also that I did not exist."

"And now," Ursula said, clutching her red pillow with one hand and thrusting the other hand up the leg of Peter's corduroy trousers, "now you are drinking too much."

"But one thing is certain," Peter said, laughing behind the leather mask of his elongated face, "and that is that Allert can always hold his schnapps."

"Any way you drink it," I whispered, "it is pure gold."

I heard the drifting snow, the poignant harmonics of the baroque recorders, Peter moving about on his hands and knees. I heard the birds collecting in their white flocks, heard Ursula humming in the random suffusion of both her comfort and her discontent. I smiled and closed my eyes. Ursula's doglike shadow was crouching above me among the beams of the ceiling. Peter was crouching at the hearth and smoking his pipe.

"But Peter," Ursula said, as I opened my eyes, "what are you doing?"

"Peter," I said in my deep and quiet voice, "are you

smearing body lotion on her underpants and not on the skin? A novel idea. I would not have thought of it."

"But it's sticky, Peter. It feels peculiar!"

Ursula laughed, Peter said nothing. Ursula made no attempt to defend herself against the handfuls of heavy lotion which Peter, as I could now clearly see, was smearing across the tight rounded surfaces of Ursula's translucent underpants.

I knelt clumsily on my hands and knees, sat back on my heels, raised the half-drained glass to my teeth. I became the willing witness of Peter's labors, since by now Ursula had returned her face to the crimson pillow while Peter, rising upward from his spread knees, had positioned himself directly in front of her, so that by leaning forward he could grip her buttocks in his two determined hands. Her eyes were closed, her head was lying beneath the apex of Peter's crotch. In his own turn Peter was wreathing his head with the smoke from his pipe and kneading Ursula's backside with his expert hands.

"It's lovely, Peter," Ursula whispered, with her eyes closed, "it feels so lovely. Like going into the bath with your panties on."

She sighed, she laughed, Peter shifted his position, I shifted mine, Peter inched forward so that he was straddling the small of Ursula's broad back.

"More," Ursula whispered, "do it some more."

One of the plastic containers lay spilled on the hearth, slowly I dropped my empty glass into the burnished depths of the water buffalo hide. The schnapps had done its night's work, reminding me of the white chateau in the village where I was born, and now I smelled the schnapps in my nose, the desert-blossom scent of the body lotion, the aromatic smell of Peter's pipe, the ice in the eaves of the uninhabited house. And now I felt too large, too sick, too purposeless, too awakened, too much in need of the lavatory to sustain my presence in our triad sprawling in the luxury of blanket, pillows, rugs, in the smoky light of Peter's fire.

The recorders faded. The darkness became to the cold-ness as light to the fire. Swaying, unsteady on my stocking feet, aware that my breathing was rhythmically focused not on the inhalation but the exhalation, slowly I groped my way down the frozen corridor toward the door not of the lavatory as I expected, but outside and into the night. My stocking feet made deep impressions in the dry snow, the flakes were settling, and all around me the winter night was invisible, a mere sensation of trees, decreasing temperature, falling snow. I stood still, I felt the snow on my head, I breathed in as much as I could of the winter night.

I thought to myself that I was in the midst of a dream that I could not remember, though my head was clear now and though off to the right I was able to see without dif-ficulty the shape of Peter's parked car humped high with snow. For a moment I saw myself as a child traveling through a clear night in the straw in the back of a little blue sleigh drawn by a black and white pony and driven by a man in a muffler and heavy gloves. For a moment longer, there in the dry snow, I contemplated what I suddenly identified as my own benevolence. And then I turned and once more felt my way into Peter's house and down the cold corridor and into that vast dark room where Peter and Ursula knelt facing each other before the fire.

They had stripped off each other's clothes and from top to bottom had smeared each other's bodies with the glistening cream. They were wet and shining, they were kneeling with their knees apart and were kissing each other and laughing. Ursula's underpants lay like a sodden handkerchief on the hearth. Their bodies were slick and moving and fire-lit as if in the emulsion of a photograph still hanging wet and glossy in the darkroom.

"Allert," she called over her shoulder to where I stood dripping and smiling beyond the light and the heat of the fire, "we've been waiting for you. Stop feeling sorry for yourself and come here and take off your clothes."

⌘

"The trouble with you Dutch," Peter was saying, "is that for you even normality is a perversion."

⌘

"You and I are fortunate indeed," Peter was saying, "to be able to rely on Ursula's sustaining sanity. She is never lost in the sacred wood as you and I sometimes are, my friend."

⌘

His voice was urgent in the darkness of the night behind her cabin door, which was hooked ajar. And recognizing his young uncultured voice from the corridor through which I was passing on my way to the ship's pool, and hearing his angry supplications and pathetic argument, it was then that I understood that all was not well with the wireless operator. With uncustomary swiftness I proceeded then to the pool where I smoked five small Dutch cigars by the light of the cold constellations.

✻

But how could I have remained unawakened by our descending anchors? How could I have allowed myself to sleep through the actuality of my own worst dream? After all, Ariane had forewarned me that we would be reaching the shores of the island in the darkest part of the night and would be dropping anchor. And it was indeed so because now the sun was rising in the lowest quadrant of my porthole like blood in a bottle, and I was wide-awake and nursing my premonitions. The ship was at anchor.

I climbed to my knees on the wet bed and opened the porthole. I saw that the sun was flooding the horizon but that the island was nowhere in sight. And kneeling with my head in the porthole and the sun in my eyes, I recalled how the night before I had refused Ariane's invitation to go ashore on the island of nudists. And squinting into the ominous and bloody sun, once more I determined to prevent our exposure to the boredom and distaste of bodies bared merely for the sake of health or naturalness.

And yet with unaccustomed haste I dressed, seized my straw hat and went out on deck in search of my young friend. The ship was silent, the gulls were gone, the hot deck might have been embedded in concrete. I tapped insistently on the door to her cabin, I assured myself that no one was enjoying the use of the pool, I understood that it would be several hours at least before juice and coffee and rolls were served in the dining saloon. The locked cabins, the empty bridge, the damp blankets heaped up in the peeling deck chairs, the silence—this, the death of the ship, was what I had always feared.

I crossed from the starboard side to the port and there against the rail were a half dozen passengers and, in the dreamlike distance beyond them, the low brown sandy island that so appealed to Ariane. I joined the passengers who did not intend to visit the island, I gathered, but who nonetheless were determined to look at those who did and, further, were hoping for a glimpse of the distant nudists. With them I stared across at the hazy island and down at the white motorboat now moored to the foot of the gangway lowered against the ship's white side.

Except for Ariane and the wireless operator seated hip to hip in the forward portion of the white launch, and except for the young crewman slouching in the stern with a rope in his hand, the long white motor launch was empty, occupied as it was by only three persons instead of sixty. I decided to become the fourth.

I descended the gangway at precisely the moment the crewman was preparing to cast off. I took my seat behind my young friend as the motor began its muffled bubbling. I glanced up at the remaining passengers propped like wax figures against the rail and under the hot sun. There was no waving, in a half circle we moved away from the high side of the anchored ship.

"Allert," she said, smiling, reaching out for my hand, "you've changed your mind."

"Yes," I said, "I too will visit your nudists."

"Without you it would not be the same."

"Well," I said, accepting and squeezing her proffered hand, "Allert also can be a good sport, as my wife would say."

We picked up speed, there was a dawn wind blowing, Ariane smiled and tilted back her head as if to take deep breaths of the burning sun. The wireless officer and I exchanged no greeting. Behind us lay the white ship, diminishing but stationary, while ahead of us lay the scorched island that was expanding minute by minute for our watchful eyes.

"I did not sleep well last night," I said. "I had intolerable dreams."

"Poor Allert. You will be able to sleep on the beach."

The sea, on which there was not the smallest wave, was now changing from opaque blackness to a turquoise transparency. Twenty or thirty feet below us shelves of white sand were reflecting the light of the sun back up through the soundless medium of the clear sea. I was relieved to notice, over my shoulder, that no smoke was visible from the blue smokestacks of the anchored ship. Ariane's hair was blowing in the wind, the long black sideburns of the wireless officer contradicted in some disturbing way the rakish angle of his white black-visored cap. My young friend in her blue jeans and a halter of orange silk, through which the shape of her small breasts was entirely visible, was an antidote to the wireless officer's unusual mood of sullen reserve.

98

"Your island appears to be uninhabited," I said, clutching the brim of my straw hat against the wind, "since there is not even one nudist to greet the eye."

"Allert," she said, "don't be skeptical. Please. There is a village on the other side of the island. The beach is momentarily concealed from our view inside its protective cove. The village and beach are connected by a dirt road which is excellent for bicycling. You must remember, Allert, that I have been here before."

I touched her cool arm and again I saw over my shoulder that our diminishing white ship lay unchanged, unmoving. I disliked the way the wireless operator sat with one foot on the gunwhale and his tunic thrown open to display the unwashed undershirt, the cross on a chain. Also I disliked his sideburns, his bad complexion, the angle of his white cap, the hand he was hiding in the pocket of the white tunic.

"My wife persuaded me, against my better judgment, to take this cruise," I said, smiling into the girl's dark eyes, "and I am not sorry. Now you have persuaded me, also against my better judgment, to journey off in a mere motorboat. And though I distrust open motorboats even more than I distrust large ships, perhaps I will not be sorry. But I am not skeptical, Ariane. I am never skeptical. I know you will take us directly to the beach of the nudists and then return us safely to our waiting ship."

But even while my heavily accented voice hung on the air, causing Ariane to laugh and the wireless operator to scowl behind an unclean hand, our motorboat veered slowly around a finger of dark sand and headed directly into a small cove that was clearly the entrance to the hidden beach of Ariane's description. The strip of pure white sand, water of the palest blue, the row of weather-beaten bathhouses like upended coffins—it was all exactly as I had pictured it from my young friend's words. The sky was an infinitude of burning phosphorus, the sand was as soft as facial powder, surely the empty bathhouses would smell of urine. The vision of the cove was familiar yet unfamiliar, I was drawn toward the listing bathhouses and yet repelled by them.

"Hurry," Ariane called the moment after our prow had touched the sand and she, in childish haste, had leapt ashore, "we really must not lose a moment of this joyous place!"

The wireless operator, in open tunic and rakish cap, was the next to jump to the dry sand where, quite unavoidable, he turned and faced me. His greasy sideburns appeared to be pasted down the sides of his jawbone. He was not smiling.

"What have you done with my photograph?" he said, with his feet spread wide apart and his hands in his tunic pockets and his hat pushed in slovenly aggressive fashion to the back of his head. Obviously he was the kind of young officer who would get drunk with ordinary sailors, abandon a ship in distress, commit strange psychopathetic acts of violence.

"I do not know what you are talking about," I said. "But I do not like the tone of your voice."

"After all, you are not the only one who needs the stimulation of an illicit photograph."

"I refuse to listen!"

100

"Return it tonight," he said and stuffed his hands deeper into the tunic pockets, and lunged off through the sand like a crazed survivor of a wreck at sea.

"And you, Allert," my young unsuspecting friend called from the bathhouses, "won't you hurry?"

I wiped my hot face on my sleeve, I began to walk slowly up the beach toward the row of narrow listing wooden structures where I, like my companions, was to divest myself of all clothing. But physical nudity was one thing, I thought, whereas psychological nudity was quite another, especially when the self was being stripped to psychological nudity by a man as ruthless and devious as the young man on whom the entire ship depended. My need was for self-control against the brutal clawing of that young man's repellent hands.

"But no, Allert, no!" she cried when I emerged from the bathhouse, "you may not wear your straw hat on the beach of the nudists!"

She laughed, standing quite naked in the hot sand. The wireless operator also laughed, though now his concentration was suddenly and unwillingly fixed on the gentle nudity of Ariane.

"What," I said, "not even an old straw hat?"

"Nothing, Allert, nothing. Not even a hat."

"Very well. But sunstroke is a serious problem, Ariane."

"But you must trust me, Allert. You said you would."

The sunlight was as intense and diffuse as any I had ever seen, the kind of sunlight that would bake alive infant tortoises buried though they might be in their thick shells deep in the sand. In the midst of this directionless glare Ariane's nude body was of the size and weight of a young child's yet it was not childlike. She was plump but at the same time thin, curvaceous but at the same time compact, and in the glare of the sunlight, which decomposed all colors to white and hence made of the island landscape a brilliant unreality, Ariane was shrouded, softened, protected in her own emanations of mauve-colored light. In the midst of our frightening white scene she alone was desirable and real. She had allowed her black hair to fall down her narrow back, her eyes were large, her small calves were shapely, there was a curious dignity in the plumpness of the small naked belly exposed without embarrassment to the wireless operator's watching eyes and mine. Her little familiar scar was hooked into the bottom of the belly like a gleaming barb, the small modest breasts and sex made me think of some overdressed Flemish child preserved on dark canvas.

Though the wireless operator was lean and muscular, while I was large and poorly shaped, still the chemical horror of the gleaming sun reduced us equally to the dead white quality of the beach itself, exposed quite equally our blemishes, our black hair curling from white skin, our genitals which in this light appeared to have been molded from cold butter. I was not pleased to find myself as unattractive as the wireless operator.

"Ariane," I said, when the three of us emerged from the path between the dunes and onto the beach, "I hope you do not find my weight entirely offensive."

"Allert," she said, and her throat was as thin and tender as a child's, "you are a handsome man."

"But tell me," I said, raising my voice and filling it with the disarming resonance of the kindly Hollander, "if a man is not used to nudism, if he is not used to being among members of the opposite sex without his clothes, in such a situation might he not display quite suddenly all the awkward aspects of sexual desire? If so, would not this lack of control be embarrassing?"

The sand was hot, my eyes felt sewn together with invisible sutures, the beach ahead of us was a glaring crescent. Behind us the wireless operator was shielding himself with Ariane's purple satchel and grunting in discomfort and disapproval.

"Allert," she said, interrupting our walk across the sand to touch my hip, to stare up openly into my wet face, "what you describe is entirely possible. But it is also natural. To me it would not be at all embarrassing. In fact," she said, more slowly and gently but also more clearly, "if such a thing occurred in my presence, I should be flattered. I should be warmly pleased."

"Thank you," I said, glancing over my shoulder at the stricken eyes, the body bent sharply forward at the waist. "Your sympathy for that situation is most beautiful. But were I in your place, for instance, and in the presence of a man who could not control himself, I would be far less charitable. In fact, toward such a man, I would show no charity at all."

"But, Allert," she said, smiling and pressing her fingers against my wet forearm, "you are a good-hearted person, Allert. I know you are."

I saw the blue of her eyes against the white of the sand, the white of the sun. And despite the fire flickering already to and fro on the tops of my shoulders, for another moment I endured with pleasure the uninhibited inspection of Ariane's soft eyes which, when they met mine, were bluer, moister for what they had seen.

"Every man is an island," I said. "I am like the rest."

"But Allert," she whispered, "you are a very special person. You are the talk of the ship."

But before I could object and point out the obvious untruth of this curious remark, Ariane reached up and covered my mouth with the smallness of her cool hand, then embraced me by flinging her arms around the enfolded fat of my naked waist and resting her head on my chest. Then she turned and with unexpected swiftness walked to the water's edge where, ankle deep in the clear undulating sea, she proceeded brightly up the white crescent of beach followed, as she knew full well, by her two naked companions, one of whom was already the color of sickening red.

"You ought to see yourself," came the voice at my back, "if you could see yourself you'd leave Ariane and me alone. A man like you shouldn't go around without his clothes. She just doesn't want to hurt your feelings. Couldn't you tell?"

I did not reply. Instead I concentrated on the sensation of the pale water against my skin and on the sight of the young woman who had thick black hair to the small of her back and who now was standing beneath the leaves of a tropical tree and waving. The island, or what I could see of it, was empty except for the eager girl beneath the tree and a far-off cluster of golden figures who, in their various sizes, suggested one of those stable families who respect the old and cherish the young and divest themselves of clothes for moral purposes. Even from this distance I noted the sweep of a patriarchal beard, the flash of a cherubic body. I looked away, I realized again that the sand of the beach was like white ash. But it was the naked wireless operator, not I, who was turning red.

"Come," called Ariane, "the shade is lovely."

Even here in the shade of the lone tree, only Ariane among the three of us looked real. Only her skin retained its natural color, only her black hair remained alive in the breeze. On either side of Ariane, where she sat upright and smiling against the tree, the wireless operator and I were merely white, except for the florid sunburn spreading like some poisoned solution across the young officer's shoulders, chest, and listless arm. The wireless operator's sallow face was wet with sweat, his head was hanging.

I held out my hand for one of the peaches which Ariane had extracted from the satchel. My hands were wet with the juice of the peach, the warm sweetness was dripping down my chin. In the distance a golden old man was tossing a golden infant into the air. And I noted in a casual glance that the wireless operator was drooping, dehydrating faster than ever, burning. If Ariane was aware of the seriousness of his condition, she gave no sign.

"Allert," she said, biting into the wet yellow fruit and unconsciously touching her left nipple as if to induce new sensation or confirm its size, "isn't that naked family beautiful? They have no shame."

I licked my fingers, I nodded. Her eyes were bright,

her armpit was slick with perspiration, on her other side the wireless operator was staring at me speechless and with dead white eyes. Portions of his slumped naked body were assuming the complexion of a fatal plum.

Suddenly I heard a thin distant voice crying, "Papa! Papa!" and at the same time heard a single fragment of the far-off mother's laughter, and at this moment Ariane and I, in perfect accord, rose to our feet and, holding hands, walked slowly to the water's edge. I knew that behind us the wireless operator was helpless and that his lips were cracked, his shoulders blistering.

The light was the color of merciless pearl, the sand was a sheet of white flame, together we rolled in clear shallow water.

"Allert," she said, stretching her little flat body beneath the water and raising her face, extending her arms and clasping both my stolid ankles, "you are so good a lover, Allert. Maybe because your mouth is so large and says so many sweet things to me."

We rose, we walked outward from the shore of the island that was as dry and livid as a glimpse of paradise preserved in a hostile photograph, walked outward until I stood waist deep in the placid water and Ariane stood facing me sunk up to her little shining breasts. The air was white, the sea was pale, all around us the air now smelled of invisible dead ash.

"We do not want the ship to sail without us," I said in a whisper.

Later, after we had performed, as I thought of it, like two unshelled creatures risen together from the white sandy floor of the sea, and after we had immersed ourselves totally in the calming waters, and after we had quit the nudist island and regained the ship, it was then that we faced the condition of the wireless operator. We eased him into Ariane's cabin and stripped him bare, discovered that the entire burned surface of his body was patterned with the clearly visible shapes of tropical leaves. Thus the wireless operator became the sick occupant of Ariane's narrow bed, and thus Ariane became his eager conscience-stricken nurse. For days the wireless operator filled her cabin with the smells of his chills and fever. For days the smell of a strong unguent filled that cabin in which there was no place for me.

✖

The sleep of reason produces demons, as Ursula once said. But I love my demons.

✖

Ursula and Peter were in the nude. Ursula and Peter were facing in opposite directions, she kneeling head down on the orange rug, he straddling her slender yet slightly aged waist and playing her buttocks, slapping and beating on her buttocks like a lean African pounding his drums. Ursula and Peter were both laughing without restraint. I also began to laugh.

✖

The lights fell on the black water as from a sinking ship. I was leaning forward, looking down, watching as the lights, which ran the entire length of the ship, began to disintegrate and sink. I heard a splash.

⌘

"Peter," I said, risking an idea I had long considered, "how is it you never married? Even now the sirens must call to you in chorus wherever you turn. Is it not so?"

He removed the pipe from between his teeth. He held the small hot meerschaum bowl in three fingers. He looked at me. And then he turned his head toward Ursula and raised his eyebrows, aimed the pipe stem in her direction, parted his lips. Then he turned again to me.

"But the question," he said softly, "is why you married. You of all people."

"No offense, Peter. I was only asking."

Again he looked at Ursula, and suddenly replaced the bit of the amber pipe stem between his teeth. Thanks to the smoke from Peter's pipe, the room smelled like a rose garden in fuming decay.

⌘

"There exists somewhere a man who wishes to amuse me, Allert, for the rest of his life. I ask only for amusement. And when I find my amusing man, I shall follow him to the ends of the earth. But we'll never marry. Never."

⌘

In my dream I am standing alone in an open second-story window on a warm day. There is not a person in sight, the trees are still, I am troubled by the fact that in all the surrounding trees and heavy foliage there exists not a single bird. But I am alone in the window and basking in the atmosphere of the tender midday sun and the slant of an exterior brown beam and an expanse of powdery tiled roof that juts into my sight above a structure that is either a carriage house or a barn. Though empty, still, even desolate, it is a peaceful scene. For a while longer I resist the temptation to look down and instead concentrate on every other portion of the warmly lighted courtyard where I find no life. Apparently the courtyard belongs to a farm complete and real except for the total absence of animals and human beings. Ahead of me stands a fragment of mustard-colored wall, the trees are green, there are motes in the sunlit air. Behind me the empty room in which I stand is dark with shadows. I am wearing a gold watch chain across my vest, I am standing in full view of anyone who might suddenly walk into the cobbled area below or who might already be watching me from some concealed doorway or crevice in the yellow wall.

Then I look down. I lean forward to rest my spread hands on the broad sill and, thrusting myself partway out the window, stare down at the tableau intended for no one else's sight but mine. I am perfectly aware that what I am looking at I must never forget, so that if my scrutiny is unemotional it is nonetheless slow and intense. I am also aware that I am making no sound, though I am momentarily moving my lips as if for speech, and that I am comfortable but quite unable to feel the slightest sensation of my own breathing.

What stands directly below my window is a large box-like wooden wagon that rides on two high wheels with wooden spokes and iron rims and is equipped not with the usual shafts for horse or donkey but with a wooden crossbar clearly intended for human use. The splintered and high-sided old vehicle remains horizontal below my window. I observe the gray wood, the heavy wooden hubs of the wheels, a wisp of dry hay caught in a joint. And what I see, what fills my mind, is the sharp-seamed and extremely narrow tin coffin which the cart contains and which is angular and unadorned except for a long single strip of fading white flowers—carnations, perhaps, or roses —stretched as on a piece of cord from the head of the tin coffin to its angled foot. The wood that absorbs the light, the cheap bright metal that reflects it, the string of near-dead collapsing flowers that divides the lid of the coffin from head to foot, instead of lying conventionally in a rich full bunch above the breast of the dead person concealed within—these are the details that make me realize that eventually the coffin must be carted away and that death is the true poverty.

But there is something still more unusual about the sight below. Feeling my brow tightening in a single crease, it is then that I see that the poor tin coffin rests not on the bottom of the old cart but rather floats in perhaps a foot of dark water. Yes, I see now that the cart is partially filled with water in which the coffin is gently rocking. And then I understand. I stare at the shining tin coffin and at the standing water and listen to my own breath and understand the reason for the water in the old wooden cart: originally the coffin was packed in ice, a great quantity of ice, which has melted.

Am I the person to pull the slow cart out of the court-yard and, lodging my stomach against the wooden bar and hearing the coffin bumping like a small boat against the wood at my back, drag this inexplicably grief-ridden assemblage to whatever resting place awaits it?

I do not know. I stand in the window. I hear the buzzing of a single fly.

When I finished reporting this dream to Ursula, who had listened with more than her usual lassitude, she made two quite toneless comments while rising, as she did so, to leave the room. She said that obviously the coffin contained the body not of a man but a woman, and that this was the telltale dream of the only son.

I sat alone for an hour, two hours, hearing the fly and contemplating Ursula's remarks.

✾

I stood in the twilight of our smoothly plastered white hallway, alert yet immobilized on my way from parlor to den or den to living room, where I had lighted a fire in the fireplace some minutes before. And in this stationary moment, caught in one of the trivial paths of domesticity in the light of late afternoon, suddenly I understood completely the nature of the atmosphere in which I was so keenly suspended. What else could it be if not the air of private catastrophe? The silence was gathering into a secret voice. The light inside the house was soft and clear with the muted quality of the frozen snow outside.

So, I told myself, our separation was no longer impending but now was upon me or even ahead of me, like a road that changes direction until suddenly it doubles back upon itself. Yes, our separation was now a fact. It was all in the silence and muted light. And just as I had expected I felt nothing, I anticipated no approaching pain, but was aware only of the perception of the event rather than of the event itself. I was aware of the silence. I was aware of the faded light.

It was possible that she had departed without farewells. Perhaps she had decided to spare me a final admonition, a final smile. Perhaps she had not wanted me watching as she tied the sash of her fur coat and drew on her driving gloves. Perhaps I had slumped into the folds of my newspaper, slipping away, dreaming of the goose that long ago had struck repeatedly at my bare childish calf, and so dozed through Ursula's disappearance from the long life of our marriage. Or perhaps she was even now taking her place in the front seat of her car alone or beside a new companion, and even now was preparing to play out all my speculations, all the texture of this fading day, in the unmistakable sound of a car engine.

I turned, I saw Peter's meerschaum pipe in an ash tray where Ursula had decided to leave it. In passing I thought the pipe was covered with a skin of dust, as if it were lying in Peter's empty house instead of ours, and in that moment and even as I was walking down the hallway toward the kitchen, I remembered what had occurred to me at the time of his death: that grief is only another form of derangement and that my innocent childhood had been filled with it.

I saw the two cold Dutch ovens, I heard my footsteps on the tiles, I saw the snow beyond the kitchen window, I saw the bright knives in their rack. Carefully, with eyebrows raised, with hands steady, I poured the schnapps into the little glass and held it up to the light. I felt that my face was expressionless, I knew that my actions were deliberate. I poured and then drank the schnapps. I leaned my cheek against the white tiles, each of which bore its glazed blue abstraction of an ancient Norse ship on a sea that might have been drawn by a child. I drank and waited for the sight and perhaps sound of Ursula's car. But there was nothing. The tiles grew warm beneath my cheek.

I put down my glass. I saw the glass sitting alone on the flat expanse of thick white tiles, I saw how the light revealed the invisible film of liquor that still coated the inside of the glass and that smelled so beautifully like yellow kerosene.

I turned, I waited. Then carefully I raised my fingers to the heavy mask of flesh that was my face. But then I lowered my hands, trembled, detected the first far-off indications of a sound which, in the next moment, defined itself as the sound of water in motion, running, increasing in volume somewhere on the floor above. I exhaled. I wiped my spectacles. I refilled the glass with schnapps. Because now I knew that the sound I heard was that of Ursula in the shower, and I distinctly heard the muffled torrents of steaming water that were already turning her wet skin pink and filling the shower stall with clouds of steam rich in the scent of Ursula's lilac soap. I tasted the schnapps. The little glass was wet in my fingers. Now I knew exactly what was lying in wait for me somewhere ahead on the cold calendar.

"I care very little about your 'victim,' Allert. She was much too young to engage my serious attention. But I do care about what you did. And if they acquitted you unjustly and only because you happened to have at your side a handsome wife, I can say nothing but that your next trial will be different. Very different." By the time she had completed her last sentence I was through the doorway and feeling my way up the darkened stairs.

✻

"Go to her, Peter," I said in the dark silence in which the two of us were lounging, "go to her and fill an old friend with enjoyment."

"That is another poor joke," he said, rising like a familiar and benevolent specter in the light of the fire, "but a good idea."

"Ja, ja, ja," I said to myself as I heard him fumbling his way toward the stairs.

✻

"Allert," she said, thrusting her soft face close to mine, "have you any idea of what you are doing? I suppose you do not. But you are destroying my romance with Peter. How dare you destroy the sweetness and secrecy of my romance with Peter? How can you be so vulgar as to read my mail?"

"I do not deserve so much condemnation. It was only a love letter. And the envelope was already open."

"And now Peter's beautiful phrases about love and friendship are lodged in your head as well as mine."

"I shall forget them all too soon, Ursula. All too soon."

But she was not appeased, and the clear snow continued to pile high on Peter's car.

✳

"Allert," Peter was saying, "has it ever occurred to you that perhaps you were once a patient in Acres Wild? Before my time, before we were friends? Perhaps in your distant and flaming youth you were once restrained in Acres Wild. What do you say, my friend, shall I look up the records?"

In answer I said I found it difficult to recall my youth. I was quite capable of recalling occasional fragments of my childhood, but of my youth it appeared that nothing much survived. But it was just as well, I said to Peter, and requested him to undertake no bookkeeper's search for what might well prove to be the notations of my obliterated violence. Nonetheless, when we next met, Peter asserted that despite my prohibition he had gone ahead and attempted to search out documentation of my unpredictable youth. But if I had ever been a patient at Acres Wild, he said, the records of that fact had been destroyed—conveniently destroyed.

"But, Peter," I said, and laughed, "Acres Wild is not the only psychiatric institution in this small country of ours."

For answer he simply trusted his gloved hands on the

wheel and turned his eyes from the snowy road and looked
for a long warm moment into my own clear candid eyes
and smiled his knowing smile.

"Why don't you get something on the radio?" he said.
"Some nice dance music, perhaps."

Obviously Peter was disappointed that his search had
proved futile.

✳

The road that climbed the hill to the zoo was lined at
every turn with bougainvillea, with succulents, with small
religious way stations pink or blue, with palm trees that
cast their rubbery shadows on horse, driver, carriage, and
we three silent passengers squeezed together on the narrow
rear seat of the black carriage. I smelled the comforting
drowsy smell of the old horse, I felt Ariane's small perspiring thigh against my own thigh. I was aware of the sound
of the horse's hooves and the turning wheels, of the erotic
plant life that bedecked our ascent and of the white tiles
and silver bells of the little uncorrupted city below. But
most of all I saw the white ship anchored and looming
down there like some nautical monstrosity in a painted bay.
The long line of the hull, the tilt of the smokestacks, the
empty decks, the sweep of dazzling whiteness, here and
there the flash of some microscopic piece of machinery—
it was a shocking unconvincing sight that justified the discomfort of the disinterested traveler in his white linen suit.
I could not decide which was less real, the ship or the plod-
ding horse. And yet with every turn of the iron-rimmed
wheels and every slow lurch of the carriage, my only urge
was to return to the desolation of the ship. So I leaned

116

forward, stared away to the east, shaded my eyes, did my best to keep our ship in sight.

We passed behind a high box hedge. The bay was concealed behind a wall of cypresses each of which was strangled in a thick climbing growth of roses. The shadows of palm fronds swept before my face like cobwebs. We emerged from our moment of gloom, the hearselike carriage canted upward. The ship was still there.

"Give me a handkerchief or something," said the wireless operator, "I've spilled the wine."

I watched the wireless officer holding the opened bottle of wine at arm's length while Ariane brushed and dabbed at the long wet crimson stain that dribbled down the full length of his tunic. One brass button was an island of gold in the vivid stain. Slowly he returned the mouth of the bottle to his narrow lips.

For the occasion of this day's excursion Ariane was wearing a purple and oddly ruffled silk shirt tucked snugly into her familiar blue denim pants. She was also wearing a pair of inexpensive dark glasses with black lenses and thick white frames that masked the small upper portion of her face and skull and hid her eyes. Between the ruffles of the partially opened blouse the tops of the naked breasts were more than usually visible, and now, as she stuffed the straw bag once more between her feet and put her hand on my knee, again I noted the tightness of her skin and the little field of freckles spread childishly across her breasts.

"Allert," she murmured above the sound of the shaggy hooves, "so silent, Allert?"

"Yes, today I am silent."

"You are displeased. But why this displeasure, Allert?"

"I dislike sight-seeing. I dislike captive animals. Today I'm a reluctant companion."

"But this is a famous, beautiful zoo filled with the softest, loveliest creatures in the entire world. Don't you take your children to the zoo?"

"We are without children, Ariane. It is one of the things I appreciate about our cruise, the absence of children."

"That is a sad thought, Allert. Very sad."

"If I had my way," said the wireless operator all at once, and passing the wine bottle to Ariane, "I'd pack the cruise with children. Hundreds of children. I love the little tykes myself."

"So do I," whispered Ariane, apparently choosing to ignore the obvious truthlessness of the young man now managing to put his arm around her slight damp silken shoulders.

"Perhaps the two of you will be able to study some infant animals while I eat an ice."

"Allert," Ariane said then, "be kind."

So I accepted the proffered wine bottle, drew my shoulder away from the young officer's intrusive hand which, I knew only too well, was applying insistent pressure on the upper portion of Ariane's arm. He was dressed in white, as usual he was slouched in the carriage with one foot propped high and his free hand lolling on the shiny black tin fender. Ariane was sitting stiffly between us with her eyes downcast and her slender wet back primly distant from the uncomfortable texture of the old leather seat. Yes, she was sitting primly and silently between us but nonetheless was succumbing breath by breath to the pressure of the wireless operator's seductive hand. I shifted again, I smelled the dust and leather of the hired carriage and the heavy aroma of the old unkempt horse.

Again the ship appeared, framed suddenly in a mass of rich mimosa. The wireless operator began to drum his fingers on the tin fender. His wine was swelling inside me like a red cloud.

And then we arrived, we reached the top of the hill, we clattered through the faded painted gates of the famous zoo. We rolled to a stop in the vast spotted shade of an army of diseased umbrella pines, and now even the unfamiliar worlds of impersonal ship and nameless little tourist city were gone. We descended from the carriage, we instructed the old driver to await our return. Ariane recovered some of her earlier glee and sped off in her tight blue denim pants and her passionate purple blouse toward the nearest cages. There was no one else in sight. There was not one child in that entire zoo, only the winding paths, the heavy shade, the dust, the smells of animal waste, the cages that always appeared empty until, after a moment or two of patient scrutiny, some small face would emerge pressed to the mesh, or some strange little body would stagger out of a heap of wet straw on gemlike feet. And overhead there was always the high roof of the diseased umbrella pines.

Ariane was fully recovered. She could not move quickly enough from cage to cage. She laughed, she sighed, she exclaimed over the curve of some pathetically small pair of dusty horns, she pressed her little tight freckled breasts to the bars. And at each cage I stooped and read aloud the Latin inscription concerning the little mangy malformed animal within.

"Well," said the wireless operator under his breath as we trailed behind our delighted Ariane down a cracked clay path beneath the pines, "well, it's just the place for an old colonialist like you. We ought to lock you up with that frigate bird over there."

I did not reply. I did not challenge the belligerence of the wireless operator. Ears flickered in the shadows, I heard the sudden hiss of urine, a small red naked face appeared ready to burst. And the straw, the rust, the scatterings of gray feathers, the piles of bare bones, the droppings, the distant cry of some furry animal, the great round luminous eyes of an old stag collapsing and sinking rear end first into a pool of slime—here, I thought, was the true world of the aimless traveler, and in this hot garden of captivity the disreputable young man at my side was at home, it seemed to me, and harmless.

"Allert," called Ariane, who was now out of sight around a curve in the path, "come and see what I have discovered!"

In another moment or two the wireless operator and I rounded a curve in the path, emerged from a sheltering screen of scaly pine tree trunks, and entered a long un-painted single-storied building of weathered wood. It was the reptile house, a fact which prompted from the sauntering young ship's officer a few more unpleasant remarks about men who assumed reptilian roles in their old age. From the entrance at one end to the exit at the other, it

120

consisted of a single rectangular room that to me suggested an old dance hall lined on either wall with unimaginative displays. The light was poor, the place was empty except for the three of us, on the dead air was a smell that I recognized at once as belonging only to the reptile houses in the zoos of childhood and, further, as having been secreted through the waste ducts of rodents and cold-blooded creatures lying in dry coils. The smell was like that of venom or urine or black ink in a context of crushed peanuts.

"Hurry," called Ariane, who was standing alone and small at the far end of the building, and who was calling to us and waving us on, "hurry, Allert, and see what I have found!"

The wireless operator joined our happily exercised companion immediately, while I in my worsening mood, angry at Ariane's unexpected display of bad taste, proceeded slowly down the length of the right-hand side of the reptile house, pausing from time to time as if seriously interested in a pair of discolored fangs or as if intrigued by the injury apparently sustained by the python.

"Come on, Vanderveenan," called the wireless operator, who was now encircling Ariane's waist with his arm and squeezing her slight laughing body against his crumpled uniform, "here's a special sight just for you!"

The approaching encounter in the reptile house was unavoidable, I knew, and so to proceed beyond discomfort or humiliation with the least possible delay, I turned from the all but inaudible piping of some desert animal no larger than my hand and rising on its hind legs like an emaciated miniature kangaroo, and took my place on the other side of Ariane, who was still laughing and still caught in the partial embrace of the young man with whom, in my presence at least, she had never been so familiar.

"Well, Ariane," I said in my heaviest tone and once again aware of the seams in her tight pants, "what have you found that is so amusing?"

"Bats, Vanderveenan, bats," said the wireless operator, laughing and jerking Ariane against his side.

"Aren't they strange, Allert? And beautiful?"

I took a step forward, I put my hands in the pockets of my linen jacket. I gave myself over completely to the lonely and unavoidable study of the bats in their cage. For the most part they were hanging black and folded in long wet clusters behind the wire mesh of their filthy cubicle, and not until now had I seen the demons of old barns and caves so large, so ominous, so ripe with latent disfigurement. For the most part the heads, bodies, and limbs were wrapped away from view inside the long stiff folds of those black ribbed wings, and yet in all their terrible bunches they were fluttering with hidden life. They stank with what I took to be a kind of anal ejecta. Without turning around, without glancing explicitly at Ariane and the young and slightly drunken ship's officer, still I detected his clumsy movement and knew that now Ariane herself was wearing the white and visored cap which, much too large for her, had only moments before been cocked at a lurid angle on the back of the wireless operator's bony head.

"Take a better look, Vanderveenan. Do you see them?"

I stood directly in front of the wire mesh. I attempted to hold my breath, as I had often done as a child in just this situation. I stared directly into the colony of sleeping bats, and did so with such intensity that I was hardly aware of Ariane, who was still off balance, stretching out her hand and touching my sleeve. How could I possibly not see what the wireless operator wished me to see? After all, the two waking bats were among the largest of that black horde. Furthermore, they were hanging head down and frontward and side by side and with their wings drawn apart and at eye level and in the precise center of that black clotted curtain that was hung in crude illusory fashion across the entire rear of the cubicle. Yes, the two waking bats, like a pair of old exhibitionists, were holding open their black capes and exposing themselves. I saw the pointed ears, the claws, the elastic muscles, the sickening faces as large as an infant's fist. Even upside down the two pairs of tiny unblinking eyes were fixed on mine. And the penis of each bat was in a state of erection.

"There you are, Vanderveenan. Two new friends."

"But they do not look unclean as they are supposed to, Allert. Isn't it strange? Don't you too find those little male creatures interesting and attractive?"

I did not answer. I did not move. Instead I watched a few sudden waves of unrest clicking and whispering through the dormant rows, and exhaled and then drew in unavoidably a deep breath. The faces of the two aroused and wakeful bats were grinning. Their penises, each one perhaps the size of a child's little finger, looked like slender overlong black mushrooms, leaping out of all proportion from the tiny loins.

"But watch them," Ariane was saying, "they are so agile!"

As if in response to her words and to her girlish voice,

in unison the two bats slowly rolled and stretched upward
from mid-body until grotesquely, impossibly, the two eager
heads were so positioned that in sudden spasms the vicious
little mouths engulfed the tops of their respective penises.
I understood immediately that this was how the two bats
must have been engaged—in the slow jerky calisthenics of
autofellatio—when Ariane first came upon the sight of
them.

Behind me Ariane made a sound of pleasure, disen-
gaged herself from the wireless operator, and with both
small hands took hold of the wire mesh. Her blouse was
stained, her small and perfectly proportioned face was
flushed as with some kind of rosy cream. On her head sat
the offensive cap.

"Allert," she said then, "see how much pleasure they
give themselves!"

"Oh," came the sudden voice behind our backs, "Vanderveenan knows all about that pleasure. You're able to do
what the bats do, aren't you, Vanderveenan?"

She turned. Her little nostrils flared. A small thick sun
began to climb from the opening in her purple blouse. Her
breath, for her, was heavy.

"Olaf!" she said quickly, fiercely. "Olaf, you may not
be cruel!"

But already I had turned away from the still unsatis-
fied and still voraciously preoccupied winged vermin, already I had turned away from the insult of the wireless
operator's hostile voice. I smelled the dreams of the coiled
snakes, in my slowness I contained the desperation of the
two bats, in my mouth I tasted the oily residue of peanuts

dropped accidentally and long ago by children who also would have been interested in the performance of the two bats. I exited. Ariane uttered a single faint cry inside the old building and called my name. But I did not answer and did not wait for her to join me, since I was not convinced that she wanted me to, and since she at any rate was no match for the young ship's officer who had abandoned his empty bottle near the python's cage and, clearly, had himself become uncontrollably aroused by the sight of the bats. In my mind I carried away the impression of Ariane wearing the white officer's cap as would a sailor's whore.

The light was the color of dry pine. A faded hair-ribbon was snagged, I noticed, on the thorns of a dry and naked bush. Everywhere stretched the shadowy landscape of the cages—empty, untended. A marble water fountain yielded not one cool drop, despite my patience. Its bowl was impacted with dead leaves. On I went in my white linen suit which, only a few hours before, had been fresh and pleasing to the touch when I had removed it from my stateroom closet. The light made me think of the green and yellow suffusion associated with the ashen aftermath of a volcanic eruption. The cages I had passed with the wireless operator appeared to be empty.

When I reached the carriage, which was now a piece of dreamlike statuary in the vast gloom, the old horse was unresponsive to my thick and well-intended caresses. I patted his nose, I stroked his withers, I spoke to him quietly in Dutch. But to no avail. As for the driver, the old man did not awake, though I put my full weight on the little iron step of the carriage, though the black carriage squeaked and tilted dangerously, though I resumed my former place on the cushioned seat with unintended clumsiness and noise. Clearly the old man and ancient animal were sleeping the same sleep in the depths of their age.

Thus I sat waiting for the return of the lovers. I relaxed as best I could, I noted the straw bag on the floor beside my foot, I crossed my knees, I smoked a cigar—but too quickly, a little too quickly—and alone in the sleeping carriage and vast silent zoo I thought with mild bitterness that here was the reality of the "Paradise Isles" promised in the pages of the brochure describing the special delights of our endless cruise. Here, I thought, was the truth of our destined exoticism, the taste of our dreams.

I nodded, I took a last puff on the cigar, I coughed, I saw Ariane approaching up the shadowed path. She was alone, she was bareheaded, she was walking briskly, she was still tucking in her purple blouse and adjusting her tight pants. It was a trivial but significant operation—the sum of those gestures—and without speaking, without changing my position in the carriage, without smiling, I read in the movement of her hands and fingers the message of what had obviously occurred on the dusty wooden floor of the reptile house. She was angry, she had dressed in haste, she did not wave to me or speak. It was only too apparent that she was indifferent to my perception of the whole long song so evident in the way she walked and the way she twisted and tugged at her clothing.

She climbed into the carriage and sat beside the Dutch corpse, as I thought of myself at that moment, and leaned forward and roughly shook the old driver's arm.

126

"We shall go back to the ship alone," she said aloud. "We shall go without him."

The startled old man took up his reins. We rode in silence. From the crest of the hills, with the umbrella pines behind us and the little silvery city stretched out below, I noted that the sun was setting like a fiery cargo on the deck of the ship. And later, after Ariane had softened, after we had dismissed the carriage, after she had followed me wordlessly to my dark cabin—it was then that she faced me and seized my arms and ran her hands up and down my arms, touching and squeezing them as if to reassure herself of what she felt for me and that I was there and real. She was small, she was standing as straight as possible and searching my eyes, her features were sponged with dark shadows.

"Allert," she said at long last and in a whisper, "please. . . ."

I heard the tenderness of her appeal, I smelled the depths of the evening sea, I deliberated, I thought of the reptile house in total darkness. And then I relented.

That night the drunken wireless operator returned to the ship supported by the two women members of the ship's band. The next day he and Ariane spent half the afternoon in the warm wind on the volleyball court.

✖

"Allert," she said, turning to me abruptly in the act of dressing, "I want to ask you a simple question." She rested her hand on the back of the leather chair and then, watching me, moving across the room, she stepped into a pair of

127

underpants which once in place looked less like a silken garment than like a faint hue that might have been spread long ago by a bearded painter. Again she paused, again she stared in my direction. I knocked the ash from my cigar. "Allert," she said then, "why are you here? Why exactly are you here? Do you know?"

But if Ursula was capable of asking me such a question, how could I possibly have been capable of finding the answer?

✼

On a morning as clear and dense with the cold as any I had ever seen, and while Ursula and I were driving down the snow-covered road in Peter's car on our way to the village, she remarked that during the trial she had had sex every night with my attorney. It was her way of rewarding herself, as she expressed it, for her loyalty. At that moment I was tempted to tell her that they had greeted me in my cabin with black handcuffs the night we docked. But I controlled the temptation then and thereafter.

✼

I awoke. I was wet. The sheets were double thick and stretched beneath me like some enormous scab peeled from the wound of the night. I could see nothing, I could feel nothing except my weight and the sensation of my own sweat laving and filming the sheets. But where had I been? What had I dreamt? Why was I so wet and stricken in clear paralysis? From what depths had I fought my way to this dead surface? Flat on my back, lips parted, waiting,

128

body slack on the sheets and wet with sweat—thus I lay alone, though next to Ursula, and thus I gave consciousness to the agony of true thirst, though my mouth itself felt thick and warm. But what had I dreamt?

Later, after I had returned to the moonlit bedroom from the blackened lavatory, to which I had carried myself like some wounded animal to the midnight water hole, and where in the tiled darkness I had turned on the tap and listened to the flow of cold water and drunk my fill, it was then that I stood in the doorway and saw that Ursula was sprawled in the moonlight with her nightdress high and her right hand undulating in the considerable erogenous zone between her spread and partially lifted legs. The heat from her body reached me in waves across the moonlit room. Even in sleep Ursula's active erotic life was not to be stilled.

But where had I been? What had I dreamt?

❋

"Well," I said, "why rock the ship? Why must you rock the ship?"

"The word is boat. I wish you would speak like anyone else. I do not find your verbal affectations amusing."

"But really it would be better if you did not rock the ship. After all, Peter had the consolation of dying in the presence of both of us. Surely one of us deserves to die in the presence of the other. Perhaps you would like to change your mind and stay. Why not?"

"You are already dead, Allert. You do not need me. I have mourned at your funeral far too long already."

Throughout this brief exchange, which was one of several, Peter's dusty pipe lay in my ash tray and Peter's automobile stood empty, locked, covered with a glaze of frost and cobwebs in our old garage. Ursula was smoking a fragrant cigarette.

⌘

In my pajamas and bare feet I entered the bathroom which was wet with steam and filled with Ursula's perfume and with another still richer smell that made me imagine Ursula milking herself into the bathroom sink. I sniffed the humidity. I gripped the edge of the sink and smelled her hair. I did not know the hour and had not even glanced out the bedroom window at the world of white snow, as was my habit. The bathroom was dark and wet and smelled of Ursula—her hair, her skin, her soap, her scent of flowers, her thin passionate jets of milk.

I turned on the tap. Nothing. I turned on the other tap. Nothing. I flushed the toilet. In a kind of fever I turned the chromium fixtures in the deep tub and beneath the goose-necked shower. Nothing, nothing at all. I trembled. I stepped into the corridor that was packed with the stillness of the morning sun.

"Ursula," I cried at last, "there is no water! What has happened to the water?"

And then I heard the sound of a car engine, and behind me the sudden furious rumbling and gushing of water in the toilet, the sink, the tub, the shower, as if my cries for peace and purification had been answered by some watery monster of indiscretion. I hurried back into the bathroom to turn off the taps.

In endless discovery of the musical imagination, I told myself, as stretched out in the stern of the ship in the folds of my canvas deck chair I listened to the syncopated late afternoon tinkling of the ship's trio. Had it been some other ship, a different journey, no doubt I would have been wrapped in a coarse blanket in my canvas chair, and the sky would have been gray, the sea rough, the air cold, our approaching destination defining without question the time of day, the nautical miles. As it was I needed no blanket and lay stretched out in the wood and canvas chair on the fantail, for no other reason than to bask in the glare of the day that had no hour and listen to the shouts of the bathers in the ship's pool and to the unstructured melodic background music of the ship's band. The music was appropriate to the day, the ship, the voyage, since it gave no indication of purpose or cessation. Without turning my head or opening my eyes I could nonetheless visualize the three musicians, and on this occasion found myself indifferent to the vibraphone player's two hands loosely wrapped in bloody bandages, and indifferent as well to the two middle-aged women, drummer and saxophonist respectively, who looked so much alike they might have been sisters.

My eyes were closed, my terry cloth robe was flung wide to the sun, our course was level, I was well aware of the tender waxed composure of my face, my cigar was aglow—and I told myself that for once I was indifferent to that foreboding trio.

At that precise instant in time, when the moment was

intact but the hour gone, I heard the reedy sentimental percussive music stop in mid-bar. I opened my eyes. The swimmers were playing porpoise in the ship's pool, the sky was clear, the bathers were shouting, far below us the engines were roughly and serenely functioning, the ship appeared real, my skin was protected from the rays of the sun by a comforting lotion that smelled powerfully of one of the sweeter spices grown on the little islands we passed in the night. But behind my back there was no music.

I raised myself forward in the deck chair. I heard the crash and clatter of what was unmistakably the sound of someone knocking over a brass cymbal loosely mounted on a long and spindly tripod. This spidery apparatus crashed to the deck. I heard several erratic beats of the bass drum. The male musician cursed—unmistakably it was his voice I heard. And then the sound of a bare hand smacking flatly against a flaming cheek, and since both of the vibraphone player's hands were swathed in his filthy bandages he, I realized, was not the aggressor. Now one of the women—drummer? saxophonist?—was declaiming some injurious message in a foreign language which to me was incomprehensible. Another crash, an odd partial scale on the vibraphone, then the woman's brutish voice also stopped in mid-breath.

At that moment, which was also unmarked in the sea of time, Ariane appeared suddenly beside my chair. As I was straining to lean around to my right and peer in the direction of the ship's trio now disbanded, silent, Ariane appeared on my left and leaned down, gripped the wooden armrest, and spoke to me softly, urgently, in a tone I had not heard before.

"Allert," she said, "the ship's orchestra is quarreling. It's dreadful. Dreadful."

Later, as the path of the ship was crossing the path of a black buoy that had been cut adrift from some unknown anchorage, and after Ariane and I had risen from the deck chair and, holding hands, were preparing to go below to her cabin or mine, it was then that I noticed the abandoned vibraphone, the silent drum, the saxophone like a golden bird strangled on the hook from which it hung, and in a heap on the deck the cymbal and its thin but ungainly stand.

"Allert," she said, "don't you think it is a sign? I could not bear a voyage that was not harmonious."

I reassured Ariane that the vibraphone player and his two ugly women were no doubt already kissing in their dark quarters below the water line. It occurred to me that Ariane had ambitions of joining the ship's trio when on the fantail they began to play their last long number as our white ship rounded the breakwater and once more entered home port—gaily, with whistles steaming and the sun in the eyes of all those jubilant travelers crowding the rail. But we returned in the night.

✼

"But of course," Peter was saying, "of course the schizophrenic has his romantic nature like anyone else. No, my friend, which one of us would dare deny the schizophrenic his possibilities for romantic behavior?"

His long dark fingers were plucking the congealed feathers from the duck that was both dead and blue. I was well aware that inside his knee-high rubber boots the argyle

133

socks were freshly bought and warm, soft, closely knitted in two colors—red and green. I knew about the nature of Peter's socks because they were mine. Above our heads the ice was suspended from the eaves like transparent teeth. The last sun was flowing across the snow.

"You should not be so hostile to Acres Wild," he continued. "At Acres Wild we have numerous long-lived affairs. It is part of the cure, my friend. Part of the cure."

That day his pipe smoke smelled like the dark forest which, only minutes or hours before, the dead duck in his hand had skimmed in swift flight. That day Peter's smile belonged on the leather face of a conquistador. The fat of the cold duck fell like red speckled droplets of candle wax into the pure snow.

⌘

To me it has always been curious that Peter, who never married, should have lived a life that was unconditionally monogamous, thanks to the power of Ursula's dark allure and her strength of mind, whereas I, who became married to Ursula one Sunday afternoon in a small stone country chapel that had hosted a funeral the same morning, have lived my life as sexually free as the arctic wind. To me it is curious that two friendly duck hunters should have been so different, and that Ursula should have thought of Peter as lover and of me as husband. I have often thought our situations should have been reversed.

⌘

Yesterday while stamping the snow with my rubber boots and burning a pile of scrub brush that I had dragged from the wall of forest that lies dark and distant behind our house, and feeling the cold air thick and crystallizing in my lungs and a new beard fringing my chapped face, yesterday I realized that between the hour of my acquittal —an event I rarely allow to consciousness—and the very moment I was pausing to wipe the soot from my jaw, there lay eight or perhaps nine long years of companionship, solitude, winter life. And during all this time I have thought of myself as moderate, slow-paced, sensible, overly large, aging. But ordinary, always ordinary, merely the owner of a small but elegant estate (with a handsome wife, with a good friend, with girl friends, with several automobiles). And yet throughout these years, I told myself yesterday while tasting the charred smoke of the fire and watching the sparks dashing upward into a dead sky, Ursula must have thought of me as a Dutch husband who had been lobotomized—but imperfectly. The medical aspect of the metaphor was one she would have learned from Peter.

At that moment the intangible again gave birth to the tangible. And leaving the fire, which was now sending skyward a long plume of smudge as though some small aircraft had just crashed at the edge of my forest, I indeed felt lobotomized. My head was like a boulder encased with ice. My steps were slow. I knew that if I could have taken a hammer and cracked open my icy rock, my frozen head, I would have found inside the perfect memory: that it now has been three years since Peter's death.

In the kitchen I found set out in the center of a stone dish my usual little clear glass of schnapps, which I seized and drank down even before removing my pullover or

washing the signs of the burning fire from my numbed
and naked hands.

"Ursula," I called, "are you here?"

There was no answer.

✳

"I do not mean to hurt your feelings," Peter was saying, "but tell me, Allert, are you wearing a wig? This evening you look exactly as if you are wearing a wig."

He swished the ice in his glass. He stretched his lean
leg toward the smoldering fire. He laughed, Ursula laughed,
I also laughed, because only moments before Peter uttered
his unfortunate remark I had been guilty of wondering
precisely the same thing about my well-groomed friend. A
trick of the light? An offshoot from our undeniable pro-
clivities toward a night of love? Perhaps, perhaps, since
Peter's hair gleamed thickly in the low light of the fire,
while from where I sat on the other side of Ursula I could
smell the scent he had applied lavishly, secretly, as part
of his bathing ritual upstairs. But Peter's remark was most
unfortunate.

My hair has always been my own.

✳

In my dream I am once again a child tall and thickset
though very young and alone in the large white chateau in
the village of my childhood and youth. The day is mysteri-
ously cast, the afternoon is indeterminate, the enormous
sleeping chamber in which I stand is not mine, in a single
slanted plane the late sun lights the room with a brightness

that will never die. And I am alone, I am unable to hear the slightest sound, neither the ringing of cutlery from the kitchen far below nor the voices of women nor the sounds of our white geese gabbling outside. I am safe, or so I believe, safe and unaccountably standing in the center of a room that is large, warm, scented with dusting powder and a skin lotion distilled from the oil of pine. The room is familiar and unfamiliar both. I know it to be the room from which I am ordinarily excluded except by invitation. And yet alone and trembling in the midst of this serenity, with the door shut and sunlight penetrating my young life in a single plane, I also know that I have not seen before this bed, this dressing table, this chair as soft as a giant peach, this soft carpet which is like a field of snow. And yet I recognize the pair of black masculine hairbrushes on the dressing table.

I am precisely aware of why I have risked entry into this large and seductive and, yes, even precious room. I know what I want. I have known about it for days, for a month, for seasons of childish need. It is an agony, a thought of joy. And standing in the center of the room, my innocent fleshly body bisected by the plane of light, and glancing at the vast bed and at the icy full-length mirror affixed to what I assume to be a closet door, again I tell myself that it must be so, that I will not be denied, that once and for all I must know with certainty what a woman looks like without her clothes, or without most of her clothes.

I tremble, I am an impresario, the director of a magical actor on a secret stage because I am all too well aware that

137

I myself am my only access to what I want to know. I smell the feminine smell of some hidden powder puff, I feel the tension in the pale coverlet drawn so tightly across the enormous bed that this decorous piece of furniture now openly appeals to me as forbidden, lewd. Yes, I ask myself, how else am I going to discover what a woman looks like without her clothes? Since the actuality is quite impossible, since I am unknown to any woman except those who live in our house (mother, two maids, an old cook), since I am young and innocent and not given to spying, even though my urge is desperate—yes, how else will I ever see what I need to see, know what I must know, if not through myself and my own ingenuity?

I am aware of the bed, the sunlight, the silence, the undergarments on the bed, the mirror occupying the entire space of the closet door. My plan has leapt to me from the silence. The mystery will be revealed.

Quickly and with precision I squeeze out of my short pants, remove my underpants and square black shoes and wintry socks and my tie, shirt, undershirt, and then possessed of myself and my brilliant plan and in agonizing control of my desperate self, slowly I approach the bed and seize the delicate lilac-colored undergarment. With care and languor and excitement I manage to put my bare feet through the holes, clumsily, deftly, and to draw that flimsy garment tightly up my childish thighs, careful not to tear the silk, with each tug smoothing the thin delicious tissue against my skin. Finally that undergarment, fragrant and lilac-colored and clearly intended for an adult woman, has become the second skin perfectly fitted to my young boy's substantial buttocks and yearning loins.

How did that intoxicating vulnerable undergarment appear so magically on the inviting bed? And whose body was it actually intended for? My mother's? One of the maids? I do not know, I do not care, at last I am touching, feeling, actually wearing what I had only seen before fleetingly in the pages of slick and sumptuous magazines. I am filled with the breath of my commencing transformation. The warmth of all the world to come is about to be revealed. The sun's plane is stationary, my rapid breath is clear.

Then I execute the final moment of my plan. I conclude my magical performance on the secret stage. Naked except for the lilac-colored underpants and smiling, calculating, swiftly I slide along the wall to the closet door, then seize the knob, and without once peering into the mirror turn the knob and maneuver the door to an angle of approximately forty-five degrees and turn, push the heavy peachlike chair to the edge of the field of vision inside the mirror. Then I steady myself against the chair and, with more care than ever, position myself so that my body from the waist down will lie entrapped but free to assume a quite different life in the silvery glass.

I open my eyes. I move my head as does a snake to his charmer's pipe. I prevent my head or torso, or much of my torso, from appearing in the magic glass. And there it is, the belly and hips and thighs and calves of a smallish tight-skinned woman wearing only a pair of lilac-colored panties in the afternoon. She is alive. She is moving. Already the elastic bands in the legs and waist are leaving little red teeth marks in the flesh of the woman in the glass. Her skin is white, it is tight and smooth, the muscles with which she is working her buttocks are entirely visible inside the transparent lilac flowers of her panties, and her thigh nearest the now ecstatic viewer is plumply raised, naturally concealing the most secret of all soft triangulations from the fixed and eager eyes of a viewer who would never have spied on a living woman but who spied with love and relish on himself.

An arm appears, a limp foot flexes into a tempting arc, the calf of the raised leg dangles in the lovely glass, the left hand travels up the calf and down the raised thigh in a tender stroking motion as if in a long tactile appreciation of a bolt of rare silk. The plane of sunlight bisects the plump waist. The small hand rests on the hip, then snaps the elastic, and then slowly appears over the top of the thigh and down to the concealed thirsting front of the underpants.

I gasp, I look away, the room goes dark in a single subdued shadow, and young boy once again, and wet with the strain of imagining, quickly I pull aside the crotch of the underpants and resting my limp back against the chair, watch as a long thin phosphorescent string shoots from the tip of my small red panicky penis and in slow motion coils sinuously across the room and floats, wafts, rises to the high ceiling where endlessly it gathers itself up in vast wet stringy loops and masses.

My little performance is over. I have seen it all. In countless forms I will see it all again. And as I sink into darkness I hear behind me the opening door and the cool comforting voice of a woman saying, "Tomorrow you must get a haircut. For a fine young man like you, my dear, your hair has gotten much too long."

One of the maids? Mother? In my new-found serenity I do not need to know.

When I recounted this dream to Ursula, she told me that if only I had had a sister I would not have had to ingest within myself the explosive Oedipal ingredients of the boy-child's life. If I had had a sister, she said, I would have been happier and would not have had to become my own mother, as well as her admiring little voyeur, in my earliest dreams. Or perhaps I should have been a girl. But then again perhaps such a spectacular ejaculation, she said, was worth any price.

At this moment the tone of Ursula's voice was atypically soothing, and in the dark it was no doubt the tone of her own voice in her ears that precipitated the tender but deliberate movement of Ursula's hand in quest of the rumpled front of my trousers. When she might have hurt me worst she pleased me most.

But how was Ursula so quick to recognize that the woman I became in my dream was my mother? And how unfortunate that Ursula could not have been always so perceptive and so humane.

✖

"Allert," Peter was saying, "do you remember our conversation about a course of treatment I finally persuaded my staff to abolish at Acres Wild some years ago?"

I smiled my heavy meaningless smile. I tapped my temple, I tried to reconstruct some faded conversation about psychiatric treatment, though why should I care, I thought, what was it to me? I leaned down, tugged at my fallen brightly colored sock, nodded my head. My study was white, attractive, well ordered but oddly filled with the overpowering stench of schnapps, though only one small glass gleamed within easy reach of my swollen and slowly drumming fingers. I struck a match and slowly puffed on my cigar. I was well aware that Peter was watching my eyes closely. I recollected with utter clarity that he had remarked repeatedly that my eyes were much too small to be trusted. In my study we were alone and facing each other in twin chairs.

"Yes," I said, exhaling, using my hands to cross one knee upon the other, "yes, I believe I do remember something of the sort. For you it was quite a victory, was it not?"

"Yes, my friend, it was a victory. Even your brightest young clinician can be fixated on the old barbaric ways. And yet recently I've been thinking that perhaps I was wrong. Perhaps that treatment should not have been abolished."

"But it was dangerous. If I remember, you said it was dangerous."

His blue eyes were watching mine. One of his knees was crossed upon the other, as was mine, and his long dark fingers were prayerfully joined at the tips. His leathery face was a mask of expressionless concentration and dead nerves, his angular elegance was a mockery of my own shapeless size. It was obvious that Peter would never know the sensation of fine blue veins treading the whiteness of a fat arm. I waited, puffing the cigar, thinking of a bay horse harnessed to a gleaming carriage behind a white chateau and recognizing the familiar seriousness, even condescension, of Peter's talk. Once again he was trapping me, I knew, in one of his dramatic pauses.

142

"Yes, Allert," he said at last, "you're right. The treatment was dangerous."

He paused. I could resist no longer the little glass of schnapps. I found myself imagining some hostile patient who, in a mad stroke of understanding, snatches from the pocket of Peter's long white coat a cheap paperbound work of fiction concerning a pair of young nurses who set about using their sexuality as a cure for maniacs. Another dangerous treatment, I told myself.

"The problem with that archaic cure," he said at last, as if lecturing some of his students in the warm light of my study, "was that by subjecting the patient to deeper and deeper states of coma we brought him increasingly close to death's door. The patient descended within himself and, while we, the worried staff, hovered at his side, always waiting to administer the antidote or undertake the rescue mission, so to speak, the patient was traveling inside himself and in a kind of sexual agony was sinking into the depths of psychic darkness, drowning in the sea of the self, submerging into the long slow chaos of the dreamer on the edge of extinction. The closer such a patient came to death the greater his cure. The whiter and wetter he became in his grave of rubber sheets, my friend, and the deeper his breathing, the slower his pulse, the more he felt himself consumed as in liquid lead, the greater the agony with which he approached oblivion, then the greater and more profound and more joyous his recovery, his rebirth. The cure, when it occurred, was remarkable. The only trouble was the possibility of the patient's death. On the other hand, coma and myth are inseparable. True myth can only be experienced in the coma. Perhaps such an experience is worth the necessary risk of death."

He stopped, paused, frowned. His dark elongated face assumed an expression of grief and profundity. But I knew that he was not yet done, that there was something further he wished to say, which caused my own breath to grow more shallow. So I myself said nothing, but, well-intended and helpless as always, merely glanced at him with my usual openness as if to beckon him on to his conclusion, his familiar bitterness. I found myself wishing for gray light and falling snow.

"Allert," he said then, as the sweat came out on the back of my neck, "has it ever occurred to you that your life is a coma? That you live your entire life in a coma? Sometimes I cannot help but think that you never entirely emerge from your flickering cave. You must know things the rest of us can never know, except by inference. But I do not envy you the darkness and suffering of your coma, my friend. I hope you do not die in it."

Silence. More silence. He was through at last. And I raised my hand, I took three puffs on the cigar, I raised my head, the glass of schnapps was empty, the room was warm. Peter was standing, preparing to stroll out of my study in search of Ursula. If pity could kill, as Ursula was fond of saying, I would have died in his glance.

"I am fond of you," I said. "Ursula and I are both fond of you. But there are certain days when I do not enjoy your company."

As he passed me he allowed his hand to rest for a moment on my slumping shoulders.

144

✖

"What do you think of my theory," Peter was saying, "that past a certain age it becomes quite impossible to make new friends? The avenue of the unexpected friend is simply obliterated. No enjoyment of sudden recognition, no new faces, no prolonged sharing of secret confidences never heard before, no thrill of a new voice in the open air. None of this for those of us who are beyond a certain age. We simply live as best we can with the old friends we have already made, until there is one offense too many or some silly eruption of sexual conflict, or one of us dies and thus even the old friends disappear. It is a desolate situation, my friend. Quite desolate."

"But, Peter," I said, laughing and in slow motion thrusting my hand through the clear pane of glass toward the falling snow of my childhood, "at least our mistresses tend to retain their allure, their interest. Is it not so?"

But I myself have never had a mistress, of course. Only my eager young girls and friendly women. Only a wife.

✖

"What do you think of my theory," Peter was saying, "that a man remains a virgin until he commits murder? The destruction of unwanted purity depends not on sexual experience but only on the commission of what is generally called the most heinous of crimes. What do you think?"

✖

My rash is now an unremovable undergarment that covers and contains my belly and buttocks and genitalia

145

in a wet palpable flush of color like a tincture of blood in warm water. Thus it has spread. But this flush, this color, is thicker than skin. It is a growth that has totally enveloped the mid-portion of my body and, in the process, has lost its pebbled texture that once brought to my mind the flesh of the pink-lipped strawberry. Now it is smooth, velvety, thick and, throughout most of the day, glistening and moist with its own secretion. I have never known such a rash and could not have imagined any skin condition capable of so much change and such determined growth. It is as if I am girdled day and night with the velvet, as it is called, that covers the antlers of those northern horned creatures (elk and so forth) in the period immediately preceding the season of sexual aggression and mating. But the sight is not entirely unattractive. And my rash does not itch. Of course the question is whether or not it will continue to expand its dominion until it covers my entire body, or whether it will be contented merely to have consumed the bulging erogenous center of my physical life.

✼

Our white chateau was bedecked with wooden shutters painted with triangular or sail-like shapes of bright purple and blue. There were geese, the remnants of a moat, a few cypress trees and a stable that smelled of ammonia and straw and roses in full bloom. Most of the cottages in the village carried our family colors on shutters and doors out of lingering sentimental deference to the time in history when the owner of the chateau was owner of the village as well. Our tulips, waxy and fat enough to fill a hand, were the pride of our old pipe-smoking coachman, who wore leather puttees summer and winter and was the driver of a small blue horse-drawn sled in which I often and happily suffered the winter cold in my childhood. It was in that sled, wrapped in a fur robe, and staring at the old man's gnomish back and at the flat snow bright with the sun, snuffling and trying to move my frozen feet, fearing the swift pace at which the pony was pulling us, that I experienced the first ejaculation of my childhood. Today I find myself hearing some of the whistled tunes with which the old coachman kept the pony alert.

When I am able to exercise my memory of the distant past, which is not often, I am able to do so with the precision of a stamp collector.

⌘

I clung to the rail. I was in the grip of the wind. The ship plunged like an abandoned freighter. The day was without light, the noise of the sea was deafening. And suddenly I felt his arm holding me tightly about the shoulder and felt his cold wet mouth close to my ear.

"Landfall tomorrow, Vanderveenan," he was shouting, "landfall and island whores, Vanderveenan. Plenty of them. Just what you need. . . ."

He tore himself loose from me and staggered off against the wind. And there at the rail, spread-legged and drenched in spray, I stood hearing again and again the echo of his hard young voice as the afternoon died away and the troughs between the waves grew deeper and the sea became vaster and blacker and louder than anything I had ever known.

I waited. I licked off the spray. I waited. In the darkness and in passing I acknowledged to myself that the ship's orchestra was warming up, faintly, beyond reach of the sea.

I listened.

✳

Deep in one of the leather chairs, feet resting on a leather hassock, half a dozen bound volumes on the rug-covered floor at my side and a single volume from the same set propped in my lap, thus I sat in complete absorption and yet also exposing myself to the fair light that always accompanies the waning day. I studied my elegant volume. Ursula and Peter sat side by side on the small white leather love seat half surrounded by some of Ursula's green plants. The plants were thriving and intensely green, Ursula was writing a letter, Peter's arm was around Ursula's waist. His eyes were closed, his hand lay with evident tenderness on Ursula's hip. The last sunlight in the room was turning the color of the stem of Peter's pipe.

"Allert," he said, without opening his eyes, "what are you reading? Why so studious?"

Hearing the sound of Peter's voice and Ursula's pen, telling myself that Peter had spoken and to me as well, I looked over the top of my large leather-bound volume in the direction of the love seat where Peter and Ursula were sitting as if for a large revealing photographic portrait in black and white. I smiled in order to acknowledge Peter's question within the silence of my concentration. In this way I was on the verge of answering when Ursula, still composing her letter with the swiftly moving black pen, spoke up ahead of me and in my stead. The snow had been falling since before dawn, but now the darkening sky was cloudless and filled with the color of burnished gold. Beyond the window the earth and pines and birches, already crusted with the frozen accumulation of other storms, were now several inches thicker with a pure illusory powder of bright snow.

"Allert is looking at his pornography," Ursula said. "At such times he is always distracted."

Peter's head was tilted backward and resting on the curved white leather surface of the love seat. His smiling face appeared to be scanning the ceiling. He appeared unconscious of the fact that he had thrust his dark fingers into the waistband of Ursula's tight slacks. He was sitting low in the seat with his legs stretched out before him and slightly spread, quite unaware apparently of the sensation of Ursula's warm thigh against his own. Ursula was sitting with her legs crossed knee-to-ankle like a man. Today the gold point of her pen was precise and furious. Her tight slacks were the brushed warm sandy color of the doe freshly shot in some wooded glen.

"Pornography," Peter said, musing as if to himself but addressing me, "does it not become boring, unutterably boring, my friend? Please be honest. I want to know."

"What a shocking thing to say to Allert," Ursula replied immediately, once more speaking for me though still concentrating on her letter. "After all, Allert covets sexual representations of any kind. For Allert almost anything representing the female or female form is pornographic."

"So," murmured Peter after a brief thoughtful pause, "so your collection of pornography is extensive."

"The work of a lifetime," Ursula answered simply. "An entire lifetime."

"And you do not find your collection boring."

"For you and me," Ursula said quickly, though in a mild and somewhat unthinking voice, "Allert's pornography would be intolerable. You and I do not filter life through fantasy. But it is otherwise with Allert. You cannot tear him away from a picture of a bare arm, let alone an entire and explicit scene of eroticism."

I rested the heavy volume flat on my knees. I valued the calmness evident in Ursula's soft face, which was broad and shadowed with golden light and turned slightly downward toward the handwritten sheets of paper gathered on the large and stylish magazine spread on her lap, and evident also in Peter's dark face which, smiling through the guise of sleep, was quietly and comfortably awake. The thickening golden light harmonized the soft white face and the face that was wrinkled, dark. Ursula had changed her position and folded her legs beneath her, as might a young girl, and she was wearing a soft tight shirt knitted from yarn my favorite color, the palest of all shades of purple. Even from where I sat I could smell her skin, her garments, her hair, her black ink. Peter was pressing his flat hand deep inside the waistband of Ursula's tight pants and had never looked more at ease, more at home.

"But my interest in pornography is not compulsive," I said then. "I am afraid it is not nearly as compulsive as Ursula tries to make it sound. Of course my interest in the entire range of depicted sexuality is genuine, quite genuine, as Ursula says."

The pen moved, it seemed to me that there was a certain tightening in the corners of my friend's closed eyes, though he continued to smile as if for the benefit of some admiring creature concealed behind the flat whiteness of our ceiling, and now I noticed Ursula's two shoes on the rug, dark brown plastic-coated shoes with silver buckles, and noticed that without turning his head Peter was clearly breathing in the scent of her purple shirt slowly and with immense pleasure.

"If you were still a boy," he said then, and not at all as if he had heard my own declaration of a moment before, "or if you were one of those poor devils always hiding a picture of some sad nude woman under his pillow, I would understand. Pornography has its purposes. I am not a psychiatrist for nothing, my friend. But your own interest is to me perplexing. But tell me, Allert," he said then, using an apparently unconscious toe-to-heel motion in order to remove his shoes which, I noticed, were made to be worn without laces, "tell me, what are your favorites? I suppose you enjoy favorite poses and activities, favorite kinds of pornography?"

"Couples rather than singles," Ursula said at once in a quick voice that was amused but serious as well. "Western rather than Eastern, photographs rather than drawings, black and white rather than color, an occasional series of women without men. Contemporary narrative, but illustrated. As for animals and women," she said then, smiling at Peter and capping her pen and removing Peter's hand from inside the waistband of her slacks, and then standing and putting aside her finished letter and reaching for Peter's warm hand, "in that situation Allert prefers dogs. Large, affectionate, but short-haired dogs."

This remark caused the two of them to laugh, as Peter raised his arm and accepted Ursula's proffered hand, though his eyes were still firmly closed, while in her own turn Ursula looked over her shoulder and gave me a glance that was both kindly, I thought, and vacant. Obviously Ursula was applying pressure to Peter's hand and arm, while Peter, without exactly resisting that pressure, nonetheless remained in the same position he had been assuming all afternoon—head back, eyes closed, legs stretched before him and slightly spread. At this moment I found myself admiring his chocolate-colored trousers and yellow shirt, which were surely a match for Ursula's beige-colored trousers and purple top. Ursula's green plants, so fresh and pale in hue and intensely green, framed them in a miniature bower that was increasingly romantic in the deepening light.

"Dogs," Peter said at last, as I myself leaned forward toward their group of two, "short-haired dogs. And the homosexuals? Have you no place for the homosexuals?"

"Allert," Ursula replied at once, "is not interested in homosexuals. Unless they are women."

"Which of course raises the question of whether or not we can put our faith in our taste. Perhaps taste is deceiving. Perhaps you have not given the partners of the same sex a fair chance."

"In these matters," came Ursula's immediate reply, "Allert can be quite rigid."

152

"So it is really true, my friend, that you think only of sex."

"Of nothing else," Ursula said quickly, laughing with curious gentleness in my direction, "of nothing else at all!"

"Oh, but you exaggerate," I said then, interrupting their exclusive dialogue and returning Ursula's teasing smile and noting the two empty pairs of buffed and glistening shoes on the white rug. "The truth is that I indulge myself only occasionally with my collection, which is an excellent one, if I may say. I would show it to you, Peter. Happily."

It was not my invitation that prompted Peter to laugh, to open his eyes, to respond with vigor to the pull of Ursula's strong hand, and to stand up at last and yawn, wipe his dark face with his free hand, and to stare down at me where I sat once more reclining and with the open volume tenting my belly, though he did these things at the very moment I spoke.

"But why, my friend, tell me why? What is this interest in the sexual concoctions of other people? Do they arouse you? Do they amuse you? But my friend, they are not even real."

"Allert's theory," said Ursula in the long pause during which she and Peter stood looking down at me hand in hand and heads together, shoulders together, bare feet and stocking feet pushing aside the empty shoes, "Allert's theory is that the ordinary man becomes an artist only in sex. In which case pornography is the true field of the ordinary man's imagination."

"Splendid, splendid," cried Peter, "you have thought it all out. But Ursula," he said then, turning and frowning

153

at her with mock savagery, "why do you not allow Allert to speak for himself? It is a habit you must break at once."

"But Peter," she said in her softest voice, while smiling at me and drawing Peter through the door and toward the stairs, "Allert may always speak for himself when he wishes."

Carefully I laid the volume, which was one of my most valuable, among the others arranged like fallen monuments on the silken pile of the gray rug. The light in the room was now so darkly golden that sight was difficult and I was not able to read Ursula's bold hand nor distinguish their lovers' footprints in the thick pile of the rug. The leaves of Ursula's plants were sharp and black, the house was still.

Outside, where I remained for a considerable time without my pullover or fleece-lined hat, the dark golden color was suffusing the frozen air with the splendor of the end of day and the approach of night, and the geese, which had become aware of my presence even from their distant vantage point at the edge of the forest, had waddled all that long way in a frenzy of ugly noise and innocence, and were pleased enough to do their waddling dance for the sake of the rich bread crumbs I flung time and again across the golden snow. Even in the darkness I stepped among them. I felt the cold in the depths of my lungs, in circles I flung the handfuls of stale crumbs and chunks of bread as far as I could. Out there in the frozen darkness, how long did the poor geese await my return?

When at last I re-entered the house and felt my way across the vast unlighted kitchen and down the hallway, and once more into the central room, where I intended to resume my reading, as Peter called it, there I discovered Peter sitting in my chair beneath the brilliant light of my chromium-plated lamp and with my rarest volume propped on his lap. Except for the illuminated seated figure of Peter, who appeared to be made of wax, the room was otherwise as dark as it usually was in the middle of the night in winter. The house was silent.

Peter glanced up from the open book. He did not smile. He was still in his stocking feet.

"Your collection is excellent," he said. "Excellent."

✳

"But a man without memory, a man who remembers not even the date of his own wife's birth, is simply a man without identity. Is it not so, Peter? And Allert remembers nothing, nothing. Not even the date of my birth."

Peter sighed, I assumed an expression of exaggerated sadness on my pudgy lips, as Ursula called them in her less pleasant moods, while Ursula again insisted that she was serious and that I had no identity. And now she walked on ahead of us, with her hair down and her hands on her broad hips.

"But, Ursula," Peter called, "why must Allert have identity? If he is kind to you, is that not enough? But of course the problem is simply that you do not always appreciate Allert's identity, which in fact is quite undeniable."

"I remember more than she thinks," I murmured then. "But I am probably too old for her. What can I do?"

"I have no idea, my friend. But you ought to remember that you and I are the same age, and I am not at all too old for Ursula."

At that moment my sulky wife was walking on the balls of her bare feet and into the sun. Peter was humming under his breath.

I began to doubt my identity. But I still had my self-esteem, which was not diminished.

❋

"Now, my friends," called Peter from the lip of the green hill, "now we shall have our feast of the sea!"

The birch trees were slender and girlish in the evening light, the hillside was muffled in green leaves, the birds in the wood were singing to the fish at sea, the smell of the flowers beyond the hill was mingling with the smell of dead crabs at our feet. And down the path came Peter, dressed in his undershirt and athletic shorts and burdened with a charcoal burner which he carried laboriously but with evident pleasure. Over his shoulder were slung a pair of long hip boots, fastened together by a rubber strap for carrying and here and there patched with red patches. He was being energetic, his calves were bulging, his face was damp. Down he came.

"But, Peter," I said, "why not let me help?"

"It's nothing, nothing. This is the last of it. We may begin. But as a matter of fact, my friend," he said, dropping the boots, hoisting the iron burner to the top of the large black rock where he intended to cook, "you are really going to do the hardest work. All right?"

"My happiness," I said, "as always."

"Yes, you've enjoyed your moments of repose. You've been sitting on the blanket with your wife, whereas I have no wife. But you and I shall prepare our meal for Ursula, for the goddess."

"Well, as you can see," I said, "she is dressed for the occasion."

Peter and I turned as one and smiled approvingly at Ursula where she sat on a blue blanket in a large space cleared of stones. A coil of golden kelp was reaching toward her bare feet, she was dressed in a simple yellow garment that was ankle length, that had no sleeves, that revealed with gauzy and intended clarity all the details of Ursula's thick but shapely body.

"You see," I said, "she is wearing her yellow nightgown. She is trying to provoke us, Peter."

"Beautiful," he cried, "beautiful! It is the dress of the goddess."

We leaned against the black rock that was like a small iron steamer run aground. We smiled at Ursula propping herself on the purple blanket with her seductive arms.

"Please," she smiled, "don't make fun of me. Either one of you."

"Never, never!" cried Peter. "We are simply going to make you drunk and give you a romantic time here on my rocky beach! But first we must have our little feast of the sea. Do you approve, my dear?"

For answer Ursula merely leaned back her head, stretched her legs, arched her back, spread wide her hands, closed her eyes. She was discreet, she was indifferent, she was in repose, she was ready, in near-nudity she had be-

157

come the obviously contented and waiting naiad of Peter's cove. She who was perpetually moist was now reclining in the full warmth of her languor. Slowly she shifted her naked thighs, and then allowed her head to sink back even farther, exposing still more the fulsome curve of her bare throat.

"But in the meantime, Peter, I may have some cold wine, may I not?"

He had already made three trips from the house to the cove, once interrupting a long kiss I was sharing with Ursula on the blanket, and now had accumulated all we needed for the meal. Six bottles of cold white wine in an enormous steel container covered and filled with great cakes of ice, several bottle openers, butter and herbs and olive oil, wooden spoons and sharp knives, and silverware, hot plate holders and a folded white tablecloth and the iron burner filled with coals now lighted and live—all this he had arranged on and about the shipwrecked rock so that in a mere instant he was able to put into Ursula's hand the requested crystal glass of chilled wine. She accepted it without opening her eyes. He turned, squatted, waved one of the wooden spoons over his array of culinary lyricism spread out by the sea.

"Allert," he said, "let's begin."

But it was a familiar ritual and I had already drawn on the rubber boots, which were too small for me, and waded up to my knees in the cold current. The day was warm, the sea was colder than Ursula's wine. Somewhere a dog was barking while above my head circled an enormous white gull that was meticulously cleansed and sparkling. With great rusted bucket in hand, and legs moving stiffly through the current, and bent almost double, slowly I proceeded forward like some great fleshly crane. Thrusting down my arm even to the shoulder, I clawed up handful after handful of large mussels glued together in clumps and swathed in mud. Yes, Peter's cove was famous for its mussels which were sweet and grew to maturity in large hard shells that were blue and black. Now in my clumsy way I was moving across a bed of mussels as large as some farmer's garden. I could feel the tight masses of the boat-shaped shells beneath the soles of the rubber boots and, as I wobbled forward against the current, pushing down my red and dripping arm, I was filled with the sensation of walking across the bones and shells of the earth's cemetery beneath the sea. I took deep breaths, the mud-covered clumps of mussels rattled into my sea-washed bucket. Out and back I went, with the horizon at eye level, the occasional wave against my thigh, elbow, cheek, and even chest, crossing and recrossing the hard living bed under the tide, until I clambered ashore dripping, cold, flushed with the pleasure of this accomplishment, and bearing the enormous crusted bucket into which not another mussel could be packed. It thrilled my entire self to emerge the wet ungainly harvester of what Peter called our feast of the sea.

At the shore's dark edge I washed the mussels. I sat on the rocks and wet the seat of my pants and scrubbed each shell, watched the mud flow off, polished each shell with the old scrubbing brush and, tasting salt on my lips and smelling the summer light on the air, became once more

159

conscious of the affinity every sturdy and middle-aged Dutchman is expected to feel with the moving sea. Behind me Peter was tending the glowing coals, I was beginning to feel intoxicated on the wine in Ursula's cold glass.

How long then the feast? Hours, it seemed to me, a gift of time. Almost immediately I myself drank the entire contents of one of the cold bottles without intending to. I savored a few cigars. Once while the great blue pot was steaming on the whitening coals Ursula asked for my hand, climbed to her feet and unsteady but laughing walked to Peter, who was wreathed in the steam, and kissed him, while Peter put down his wooden spoon, reached his hands behind Ursula's back and raised her yellow skirt until in the rear it was bunched into the small of her back while in front it still grazed her ankles. In that position Peter fondled Ursula's nudity until she returned to the blanket and he, drenched in the best of humors, returned to the preparation of the meal.

He steamed the mussels, he seasoned them, I heard the clatter of a wire whip, I smelled the aroma of cold tide and aromatic herbs, and the day began to dissolve in butter, wine, steam, laughter, the clanging of the abandoned blue kettle rolling down the rocks, the hiss of the coals, the showering light of the wine as it fell in an arc from the mouth of another opened bottle to a waiting glass. Together we sat on the blue blanket, dipping each opened shell into the little tubs of melted butter and sucking in the golden mussels and licking our fingers, smearing our cheeks with the rich butter, tossing empty shells and now and then a limpid mussel or chunk of bread to the white gull that was standing on a nearby rock like the fourth in our party.

Minute by minute the day dissolved into its bright shadows. Ursula insisted upon feeding us, first Peter and then me, by holding a slippery mussel between thumb and first two fingers and then thrusting it against our lips and into our waiting mouths. The mussels were sweet and flavored with the depths of the sea. Peter remarked that they were ovular. The gull stalked along the top of the shipwrecked rock amidst cloves of garlic, crushed barnacles, flakes of the rusty iron, kernels of pepper. Below him we were lying in the wash of our own debris.

"Where's my romantic time, Peter? Is this all I get?"

Ursula lay on her back with her arms drawn loosely upward like those of a ballerina. One knee was raised, the lower edge of the yellow skirt was gathered so as to barely drape the pubic shadows. Her eyes were open and to me her stomach looked invitingly rounded as a result of her unstinting meal. Peter had provided chocolates and even these she had eaten.

"Peter? Is this all?"

I leaned forward and with my handkerchief wiped a large oily smear from Ursula's cheek. The gull stood still, no longer pacing in stiff dignity the top of the rock. Peter rolled to his knees and unbuckled his belt. I smiled and climbed to my feet.

"Allert," Ursula said then, "where are you going? Don't leave us. I want you to stay."

I smiled down at her where her soft lower body was already in motion though Peter had not yet removed his athletic shorts and though she was looking not at him but at me.

"But I must relieve myself," I said in my heaviest accent. "But I will not be far off. And I will return soon. Besides," I added, preparing to step carefully between the stones, "I have already witnessed this scene a good many times, my dear. Have I not?"

"But you enjoy it, Allert. I know you do."

And so I did ordinarily. But for now my interest lay only in the narrow sun-struck path that climbed along the edge of the birches and then among the birches, and in another instant I was ascending the path in a stride that was slow and free, though now and then interrupted by a gentle stagger. My modesty was always amusing to Peter and Ursula, but I had no recourse but to follow my own inclinations and withdraw from time to time into a dark corner, a closet of green ferns. So midway up the hill I relieved myself, peered toward the island that long ago had broken free of Peter's shore, and then sat down, lay down, rolled over, dozed. When I regained consciousness, sitting with my back against one of the tilting birches, I was fully aware that I had dreamt a short concise dream about Ursula exposing her breasts at a party. It was a fleeting dream and not worth reporting to Ursula.

When I returned to the scene of the meal, a scene now cast in the warmest of shadows, I found Ursula lying in the center of the white tablecloth we had spread on the blanket and Peter sitting cross-legged on top of the black rock. Ursula's yellow gown had become her pillow, Peter was naked and sitting with his eyes closed and holding in his lap one of the sweating unopened bottles of cold wine.

The gull was perched defiantly on Peter's castoff athletic shorts. Ursula's eyes were also closed and she and Peter were smiling.

"Come," I said quietly, "let me open the wine."

Some kind of telepathic understanding rippled down the length of Peter's bare side and with effort he raised his arm and extended the bottle. I drew the cork and, filling a much-used glass, carefully placed the brimming glass in Peter's listless hand. He nodded. He did not open his eyes.

"Drink it, Peter," I said. "The party is not done."

He nodded, he made no move to raise the glass from his loins to his lips. So I shrugged and removed my shirt and trousers, took a few puffs on one of the little cigars, standing for those moments with my forearm resting in the small of my back and a foot raised on a boulder of quartz, and eyes looking down at Ursula. Then I threw away the cigar, in the process offending the brave gull, and walked to the blanket.

Later, much later, she pushed me off with brusque but loving hands. We lay on our backs, side by side. I smelled the golden snake of kelp, without looking I knew that the little black islands were knocking against each other and moving in our direction.

"I hurt," she murmured, easing the crumpled yellow gown between her legs. "Thanks to my two selfish friends I hurt in my crotch."

But she was smiling. A moment later, when Peter called my name, I used my elbows and raised my head and shoulders and saw that his eyes were open and filled with light.

"I tell you, Allert," he called, "your sexual organs reminded me of the armored bulge of one of the better-endowed British kings. How's that for a compliment, my friend?"

"I thought you were dozing," I answered. "I did not know you were watching."

"But yes, indeed," he answered and raised his glass, "indeed I was watching."

For our return to his home, Peter draped himself in the white tablecloth on which we had feasted. A mere ten days later Ursula was planning my trip in her cruelest mood.

⌘

We spend most of our lives attempting in small ways to know someone else. And we hope that someone else will care to peek into our darkest corners, without shock or condemnation. We even hope to catch a glimpse of ourselves, and in this furtive pursuit we hope for courage. But on the brink of success, precisely when a moment of understanding seems nearest at hand, and even if the moment is a small thing and not particularly consequential, it is then that the eyes close, the head turns away, the voice dies, the surface of the bright ocean becomes a sea of lead, and from the very shape we know to be our own there leaps a man-sized batlike shadow that flees or crouches to attack, to drive us away. Who is safe? Who knows what he will do next? Who has the courage to make endless acquaintance with the various unfamiliar shadows that comprise wife, girl friend, or friend? Who can confront his own psychic sores in the clear glass? Who knows even where he is or where in another moment he may find himself? Who can believe in the smoke from the long clay pipe, the beer in the tankard?

Who then is safe? I wish I had known my wife and friend. I wish they had known me. I wish we had been only dark figures within a gilded frame. Like a child I wish we had found each other tolerable. I used to wish that I could have cleaved Peter down the length of his back and pulled the halves apart as though they had belonged to a gutted dummy and then climbed inside. If I had been able to enact this fantasy when I wanted to, I would now be dead. All speculations, like loose phosphorescent threads shot dreamily into a cold night, would be at an end.

Who is safe?

⌘

In my arms she was like a small child struck by an auto. Together in the dark we swayed on the deck as if I had just dragged her from a wreck at sea. I was holding her horizontally in both my arms. Her eyes were glazed, she refused to speak. The white officer's cap had fallen from her head only a moment before, the white tunic fell open from her nude body like the remnant of some outlandish costume for a masquerade, which indeed it was. She was limp but watching me, though the eyes were glazed, and she refused to speak. The moon was a streak of fat in the night sky. I could not feel her weight. I heard a shout. I turned. I heard a splash. The deck was a hard crust of salt. The night was cold. I heard the splash. I could not feel her weight. And then along the entire length of that bitter ship I saw the lights sliding and blurring beneath the waves. Clumsily, insanely I wrestled with a white life ring that bore the name of the ship and that refused to come free. I saw the ship's fading lighted silhouette beneath the waves.

Who is safe?

⌘

"Look," cried the purser, "the horse has two rumps and six legs! Shall we give the prize to this happy monster?"

The crowd, which packed the midnight saloon, dancing and tangling themselves in clouds of confetti and streamers of bright paper, cheered in a polyglot of affirmation. I recognized the drunken purser with distaste, in my arms my little partner was wearing her bikini, the white officer's cap at a rakish angle and, with sleeves rolled to her fragile wrists, the official white tunic with its gold buttons and lightning bolt at the collar. Her small dark face looked like a child's. The dance floor was awash with gin. My partner was impersonating a wireless operator, while I (with distaste, with severity, with self-consciousness) was impersonating a heavy-set and class-conscious burgher from Amsterdam. I wanted to slip my wet hands inside the tunic.

"Allert," she cried, dragging me to the edge of the crowd where the purser was hanging a lopsided floral wreath around the horse's neck, "look, it's Olaf!"

And there he stood, now holding the horse's head in his arms and grinning. And there too stood the ship's

166

drummer and the ship's saxophonist, two coarse and grinning women exposed now from the deformed horse's unzippered double rump. For a moment longer they demonstrated how they had crouched and swayed and danced, one bony woman to each rump. At the purser's insistence the wireless operator, now wearing the ring of flowers around his own naked neck, lavishly and drunkenly kissed them both. The crowd cheered, my partner clapped her hands, the vibraphone player smeared his silvery instrument with congealed blood.

"Kiss me, Allert," she whispered, wiping my brow and fixing my tie. "I am enjoying this party so much. I want you to kiss me. Right here. Right now."

Who is safe?

⌘

When the divers descend and open up this unfortunate ship, I thought, they will find all the drunken passengers packed in confetti and paper streamers tangled like dead rainbows. The ship will be rusting, but the travelers will still be packed together in silent joy. All of them will be preserved in kelp and seaweed and bright paper—a dense and soggy conglomerate which will be to the sunken ship as the marrow is to the broken bone.

Who is safe?

⌘

I now think without doubt that I, the old Dutchman dispossessed of the helm, am the living proof of all of Peter's theories. Or almost all. Yes, I tell myself that I am the legacy of my friend, my wife's lover, our psychiatrist. Yes, I am that dead man's only legacy. But unwanted legacy, I suddenly correct myself, *unwanted* legacy. Of my friend Peter but also of the women I have known.

In the darkness I am their entire legacy, the filthy sack of their past and mine. And unwanted, every drop of it.

✳

"Ursula's complaints are meaningless," Peter was saying, "quite meaningless. You must simply ignore them. Most wives complain about their husbands. As a matter of fact, my friend, if you were not as emotionally strange as you are, Ursula would not like you at all. A curious paradox but true. And you will note," he said, smiling up at me with the wind in his face, "you will note that I did not say 'sick' but merely 'strange.' I will not pin you down, to use a vulgarism, until you request me to do so, professionally."

His long dark fingers continued to stuff the little white bowl of his pipe with shredded tobacco, the sun was a cold ray in a dark sky, his smile belonged not on his weathered and sardonic face but rather on the little round sculpted face of some clever cupid. He continued to stuff the white pipe. I removed the shells from my gun.

"But what is so wonderful and so hard to believe," Peter said then through the clarity of the fierce wind, "is that she cares for us equally. To her all our differences are nothing. And what a capacity it is to be able to elevate two such different men to the same level of acceptability. She has the gift of love, my friend. The gift of love."

Cupped in his two dark bony hands, the flame of the

168

match was pale beside the intense red color of his hunting shirt. Then the pipe was lit and the two of us, side by side and thinking in our different ways about Ursula's love, were heading home.

⌘

He bolted forward from the bench. In the dry and desperate heat, in which the three of us had been reposing as if in a dream, naked and white and at our ease, suddenly Peter bolted forward from the wooden bench and, in complete silence, flung his hands to his chest and looked around him with eyes filled with the joy of extreme pain. His chest was a network of small bones, every hairy filament in his public growth appeared electrified, his white legs and arms were long and oddly muscular, his nipples were dark, his loins were a nest of blue veins.

"Peter," Ursula said in alarm, "what's wrong? What is the matter?"

Her sentence was the only one spoken from that moment forward in the sauna. And yet throughout that terrible ensuing time, during which Peter pantomimed his death and Ursula and I our helplessness, through all that time, which on the clock was nothing, I heard Peter's voice (jocular, lofty, confidential) inside my head. As we watched, moved, tried to assist him, and while he lurched and staggered about in the small circle of his dying, I thought I was listening to every word he had ever said, and I did not know which was worse, the brief and wordless struggle of our performance there in the sauna, or the confidence and unbroken flow of that silent voice. There he was, talking

169

away at the moment of his own painful death (which was from his heart, I realized at once) and in complete ignorance of the advice, the pronouncements, the elocutions of middle age, the sparkling tones. He talked to me even after he lay dead on the floor. I could not bear to listen.

When he fell, tall white fishlike man I no longer recognized, I could hear his nose breaking on the slats. He lay on his stomach lurching and trying to crawl after the trail of bright blood that flowed from his nose. A moment before, and in shock and ignorance, I had seized his arm and attempted to steady him. But as he collapsed he tore loose from my grip. Now we could hear the very sound of the pain inside his chest.

Ursula was kneeling at his head with her face constricted, her breasts in a chaos of motion, her breathing heavy, and had somehow managed to lift his head and was now holding his bleeding head in her two hands. At his mid-section I too was kneeling, one knee raised, the other burning on the wooden slats, and I heard the faint popping sound of the tubes that were parting inside Peter's chest.

His body looked like dry fat and cartilage. He looked like a creature that had been skinned. He was still flicking with movement. But then that awful movement ceased. He was dead.

And then he defecated. Yes, even while Ursula rocked his head and tried to soothe the contorted face, and even while I knelt helplessly at his side, listening to my friend's silent voice, suddenly Ursula and I knew simultaneously what had happened and together stared in shock and grief at this last indignity.

He was dead. The smell was strong. We could not move. We did not know what to do. The fecal smell of Peter's death was overpowering the smell of eucalyptus that was filling the small room. I thought that Ursula and I would soon die like Peter there in the heat. But I could not allow my friend's body to remain unclean, that much I knew.

In another moment or so I acted on that lingering knowledge, and using my flat hand as a trowel, slowly scooped the terrible offending excrement from Peter's corpse. And bearing in my hand the last evidence of Peter's life, I managed to gain my feet, open wide the door and stumble to the edge of the cold and brackish sea.

As I hurried up the path toward the house and telephone, naked and stumbling and in my own way deranged, I thought that my hand would be forever stained with the death of my friend.

Moments later, and after I had placed the useless telephone call, I was joined at the house by Ursula, who, draped in a towel, looked at me with an expression of terror and fury and collapsed in my arms.

❡

They fished aboard an infant octopus that was already dead. The sea was in steady motion beyond my porthole as if someone had at last discovered our destination. A sailor hung the infant octopus outside my door. The motion of the passing sea was swifter than at any time during our journey. The sea was dark, the sky was exactly right for a holiday. I could hear the swishing of a few dumpy women still playing their deck-board game with sticks and pucks. Now we were on course to a destination. The impartial sky was chilly, bright. But they told me I was confined to my cabin, as if I were an officer instead of mere passenger, and accused of a crime. They told me the wireless operator had been relieved of duty and was under sedation. They told me they had spent the entire day searching the ship from top to bottom, fore and aft. But to no avail. They had looked in the cabins, the lifeboats, the engine room, the companionways, the lockers, the wireless shack, the crevices beneath the flywheels of great machines. But to no avail.

The purser was sitting on a wooden chair outside my door. His trousers were freshly pressed. We were a mere speck in the empire of that dark sea. The purser called to the attention of strolling passengers the baby octopus white and swaying on its length of cord.

They assured me that the search throughout the ship was continuing.

✳

The islands became more numerous. They were small and golden, each one a perfect bright sphere for exploring. But I was confined and he was heavily sedated.

Even inside my cabin I could hear the rumors. And a few dumpy women with wooden sticks and pucks.

✳

"Allert," she said quietly and behind my back, "it is not necessary to wash my underpants. You are always kind to me. But you shouldn't bother to rinse my panties."

172

"Oh, but it is nothing," I said, and felt the life of the ship in the soles of my naked feet. "It is an unfamiliar chore for me and one I like. But surely if you can press the clothing of the ship's crew it is somehow appropriate that I rinse your panties."

Sitting as she was on the far end of her rumpled berth, small, indifferent to the hour of the day, Ariane was not within range of the small mirror fastened above the porcelain sink. I could see the familiar disorder of the little stateroom whenever I glanced from the frothy sink to the mirror, and even had a splendid reflected view of the opened porthole above the berth, but I could not see Ariane and could only assume that she had already removed her bathing suit as I had mine. At the sink I stood with a towel knotted around my waist but assumed that Ariane would not care to wrap herself in towels.

"Well, you are doing a very thorough job, Allert," she said behind my back. "But don't you want to hurry a little?"

"Two more pairs to go," I said into the empty mirror that was quivering slightly with the pulse of the ship. "Only two pairs. And do you see? They look as if they belong to a child."

"But, Allert, I think you have become a fetishist!"

"Oh yes," I said heavily and raised my face to the glass. "Yes, I am a deliberate fetishist."

I nodded to myself, I submerged my hands to the wrists and scrubbed the little shrunken garment that felt as slippery as satin on a perspiring thigh. I was enjoying myself, half naked before the sink and rinsing Ariane's six pairs of off-white panties. They were not new, those panties, and the crotch of each pair bore an unremovable and, to me, endearing stain.

"There. You see? I am done. Now we shall hang them to dry."

But that day Ariane's wet undergarments on which I had worked with such prolonged and gentle satisfaction, remained in a damp heap in the porcelain sink. In a single instant I forgot all about Ariane's damp panties (reminding me of the clothing shop windows into which I used to peer as a youth in Breda), because in that instant I turned from the sink to find that she had not resorted to a warm towel, as I was convinced she would not, but also that there on the other end of the rumpled bed, with the wind in her hair and her legs drawn up and crossed at the ankles, she was far from that complete state of nudity in which I had thought, even hoped, to find her. But I was not disappointed.

I did not know how to respond, I felt a certain disbelief and breathless respect. But I was not disappointed. Because Ariane sat before me girdled only in what appeared to be the split skull and horns of a smallish and long-dead goat. It was as if some ancient artisan had taken an axe and neatly cleaved off the topmost portion of the skull of a small goat, that portion including the sloping forehead, the eye sockets, a part of the nose, and of even the curling horns, and on a distant and legendary beach had dried the skull and horns in the sun, in herbs, in a nest of thorns, on a white rock, preparing and polishing this trophy for the day it would become the mythical and only

174

garment of a young girl. What was left of the forehead and nose, which was triangular and polished and ended in a few slivers of white bone, lay tightly wedged in my small friend's bare loins. The goat's skull was a shield that could not have afforded her greater sexual protection, while at the same time the length of bone that once comprised the goat's nose and hence part of its mouth gave silent urgent voice to the living orifice it now concealed. The horns were curled around her hips. On her right hip and held in place between the curve of the slender horn and curve of her body Ariane was wearing a dark red rose. I recognized it as one she must have taken from the cut-glass vase of roses that had adorned our table for the noon meal.

"Allert," she said at last and into my puzzled and admiring silence, "how do you like my costume for the ship's ball?"

Slowly I shook my head. The bikini made of bone and horn was the ultimate contrast to the hidden and vulnerable sex of my young friend. I now felt that the towel around my waist was a vain and undeniable irritant.

"Yes," I said gently, "you are Schubert's child. Who but my Ariane would fuse her own delicacy with the skull of the animal Eros? And the rose, the rose. It is a beautiful costume. Beautiful. But it is not for the ship's ball."

"But I promised the purser, Allert. What can I do?"

"You may cease your teasing right away."

"Very well, my poor dear Allert. I have been teasing. I will attend the ball dressed as a ship's officer. Are you satisfied?"

"Completely," I said then, dropping my towel. "Completely."

I sat beside her on the berth. I removed the rose. I seized the two horns and smelled the dark and living hair and the tangled sheets and the sea breeze. Gently I tugged on the horns until they came away from her with the faintest possible sound of suction. I could not believe what the goat's cranial cavity now revealed. The goat's partial skull fell to the floor but did not break. I smothered my small friend in my flesh, a huge old lover grateful for girl, generosity, desire, and the axe that long ago had split the skull.

To be wanted in such a way, what was there more?

Later, as Ariane knelt with head and shoulders thrusting through the porthole and as my spread fingers straddled her shining buttocks, like a thick starfish squeezing still to know the sensations of her youthful flesh, it was then that I begged Ariane not to attend the ship's ball. I did not know why, I told her, changing my position and placing the great side of my face against her buttocks, but I felt a definite preference that she not attend the ball. Why dress, I asked, why leave her cabin? We would only become involved in a drunken frolic. Why not stay below and, if we wished, listen to the night's music through the porthole?

But she insisted.

⌘

"Why? Why? Why?" she was saying. "Why must you always try to mythologize our sexual lives? Why don't you come to my bed and have sex and stop dreaming?"

"But, Ursula," I said, frowning and climbing up from the chair, "I am merely trying to articulate the sensual mind. I do not mean to offend you."

"You are naïve, Allert, naïve. If I punch your side I will smell only a puff of smoke from a cigar. You are the least sensual person I have ever known. There is a difference between size and sensuality."

She left the room. Through the glass of the window I could smell the snow in the night. I regretted that I had offended Ursula.

✳

The infant octopus hung like the carcass of a young girl in the sun.

✳

"Allert," she called, "will you come?"

It was then, while staring through the clear window glass at her small white English auto parked in the snow, that I realized that I was to be invited after all to share in the ritual of her departure. And nothing was as I had imagined it, since she was taking her own car and not Peter's or our family sedan, and since it was dawn, and since there was no man behind the wheel of the waiting car, and since she was making no mystery of her departure.

"Allert? Will you come?"

When I climbed the stairs, corpulent and wrapped in my dressing gown, I found Ursula surveying for a final time the scene of her room. Her luggage, consisting only of a handbag, a small suitcase apparently made of the softest lambskin, and something that looked like a soldier's duffel bag and made of the same material, lay at her feet in the simplest order. She was wearing white slacks, a red knitted top, a red kerchief to protect her hair in the little open car, and driving gloves the same color as the luggage.

"Well," I said, "why are you leaving? I mean, why are you not forcing me from the house and keeping the house and cars to yourself? Is that not the usual thing to do? You needn't be generous on my account. I should think in this situation you would appreciate the reassurance of the familiar home."

"If I need anything," she said in a gentle voice, "I will telephone."

I noticed that she had made up her fulsome lips and that her white pants were extremely tight and trim. I had known her in every way yet not at all. Now she was dressed as I had never seen her for traveling, and already she was distant, attractive, strange and busy in the very room that was still filled with the confusion of her dormant nature. Evidently she was indifferent to the unmade bed, the quilt and satin nightgown kicked to the floor.

She said that she had already eaten her roll and drunk her coffee. She was simply not the Ursula with whom I had lived so many years.

She slung the handbag from her shoulders, I took the luggage. Outside it was much too cold for an older man in his dressing gown, but I stood there until she drove from sight.

She sat behind the wheel with the red kerchief already blowing and her luggage in the small back seat.

178

"You will be cold," I said. "Where's your jacket?"

She shook her head, she started the engine which to me was suddenly familiar, terribly familiar, and sounded much too big for the little car.

"Where are you going? Please, you must write me a letter."

She shook her head, she smiled, she put the car in gear.

"Don't worry," she said then, smiling up at me and speaking over the noise of the engine, "you will find some-one. You will find some nice young thing to hear your dreams."

And then she drove off. Perhaps she was simply trying to follow my own footsteps. But she would not return.

⌘

Perhaps I should commit myself to Acres Wild. Perhaps I should go in search of the village of my youth and childhood. Or I could ask the international telephone operator to locate Simone. Or I could lock myself in Peter's frozen car and submit to asphyxiation, in which case I could no doubt join my departed friend on the island of imaginary goats. But I shall do none of these things.

Instead I shall simply think and dream, think and dream. I shall dream of she who guided me to the end of the journey, whoever she is, and I shall think of porridge, leeks, tobacco, white clay, and water coursing through a Roman aqueduct.

⌘

I am not guilty.